# PAVING THE SEA



*Middle East Literature in Translation*
Michael Beard and Adnan Haydar, *Series Editors*

**Select Titles in Middle East Literature in Translation**

*Castigation*
Sultan Raev; Shelley Fairweather-Vega, trans.

*The House of the Edrisis: A Novel, Volume One*
Ghazaleh Alizadeh; M. R. Ghanoonparvar, trans.

*The House of the Edrisis: A Novel, Volume Two*
Ghazaleh Alizadeh; M. R. Ghanoonparvar, trans.

*The Man of Middling Height*
Fadi Zaghmout; Wasan Abdelhaq, trans.

*The Pulse of Contemporary Turkish: Poems from the New Millennium*
Buğra Giritlioğlu and Daniel Scher, eds.; Buğra Giritlioğlu, trans.

*Salt Journals: Tunisian Women on Political Imprisonment*
Haifa Zangana, Christalla Yakinthou, and Virginie Ladisch, eds.;
Katharine Halls and Nariman Youssef, trans.

*Tracing the Ether: Contemporary Poetry from Saudi Arabia*
Moneera Al-Ghadeer, ed.

*We Never Swim in the Same River Twice*
Hassouna Mosbahi; William Maynard Hutchins, trans.

---

For a full list of titles in this series,
visit https://press.syr.edu/supressbook-series
/middle-east-literature-in-translation/.

# PAVING THE SEA

RASHID EL-DAIF

Translated from the Arabic by
Nicholas R. Lobo and Alfred J. Naddaff

Foreword by
Zeina G. Halabi

Syracuse University Press

Content advisory: This book contains mentions of sexual assault. Please read with care.

This book was originally published in Arabic as *Tablīṭ al-Baḥr*
(Bayrūt: Riyāḍ al-Rayyis lil-Kutub wa-al-Nashr, 2011).



Syracuse University Press
Syracuse, New York 13244-5290



Published 2026

26 27 28 29 30 31 6 5 4 3 2 1

ISBN: 9780815612230 (paperback)
9780815657972 (e-book)
9780815658115 (PDF)

Publication grant generously provided by Halil Yenigun, Sohaib and Sara Abbasi Program in Islamic Studies, Stanford University Global Studies.

For a listing of books published and distributed by Syracuse University Press, visit https://press.syr.edu.

**Library of Congress Cataloging-in-Publication Data**

Names: Ḍaʻīf, Rashīd author | Lobo, Nicholas R. translator | Naddaff, A. J. translator
Title: Paving the sea / Rashid El-Daif ; translated from the Arabic
by Nicholas R. Lobo and Alfred J. Naddaff.
Other titles: Tablīṭ al-baḥr. English
Description: Syracuse, New York : Syracuse University Press, 2026. |
Series: Middle East literature in translation
Identifiers: LCCN 2026025390 | ISBN 9780815612230 paperback |
ISBN 9780815657972 epub | ISBN 9780815658115 pdf
Subjects: LCSH: Zaydān, Jirjī, 1861–1914 | LCGFT: Historical fiction | Novels
Classification: LCC PJ7820.A46 T3313 2026
LC record available at https://lccn.loc.gov/2026025390

The authorized representative in the EU for product
safety and compliance is Mare Nostrum Group B.V.,
Doelen 72, 4831 GR Breda, The Netherlands.
gpsr@mare-nostrum.co.uk

# Contents

# Foreword

## *Rashid El-Daif and the Parody of Consciousness*

Zeina G. Halabi

The Nahda, the nineteenth-century awakening also known as the Arab Enlightenment, was never simply a historical event. It was, rather, a cultural and intellectual movement that sought to engage with European ideas while revitalizing Arabic heritage. It sparked major reforms in language, sciences, and religious thought that have defined the modern Arab world for the last two centuries. Its thinkers searched for coherence in a world newly fractured by the pressures of colonial intrusion, the weight of translated texts and traditions, and Eastern/Western epistemic asymmetry.

Chief among Nahda thinkers is Jurji Zaidan (1861–1914). Originally from Beirut, a peripheral city in what was then Greater Syria in the Ottoman Empire, Zaidan imagined that reason could reconcile revelation, that knowledge could deliver Ottoman subjects from the burdens of tradition. Yet, since its first articulation, the Nahda carried the shadow of its own contradictions. Its enlightenment unfolded in borrowed vocabularies; its language was already a practice of translation, its confidence born estranged.

What begins as estrangement at the turn of the nineteenth century will morph into alienation in the second half of the twentieth century. Historical tides that began with the 1948 Nakba and the 1967 June War, all the way to the Lebanese Civil War (1975–90) and the Gulf War, bore epistemological and aesthetic implications and a collective intellectual introspection about what modernization means and what it entails. At each of these major historical junctures, thinkers and writers were left struggling with a paradox: the impossibility of fully appropriating the edicts of the Nahda and the impossibility of eschewing them entirely.

In Lebanon, where Rashid El-Daif (b. 1945) was born, such ambivalence was amplified by the unfolding of the civil war. It was a pivotal era in which intellectuals who identified with the ethos of the Nahda began questioning their prevailing modernist convictions. Those, like El-Daif, who had espoused a firm belief in binaries such as tradition/modernity, theory/praxis, or retrograde/progressive were the most transformed by the collapse of ideological referents and the growing anomie of the civil war. It was a moment of introspection, of looking at what caused such collective doubt and abysmal loss of the self. And so intellectuals reexamined their primordial ties—not as critics and rebels, but, this time, as disenchanted subjects reckoning with the angst of having ruptured traditional structures of identification, of having contributed, tragically so, to their own alienation.

It is this tragic sensibility that drives El-Daif's fiction. Emerging from the debris of Lebanon's civil war, El-Daif has produced a corpus that chronicles the slow disintegration of faith in ideology, in revolution, in love, and, most devastatingly, in literature itself. His novels are about disoriented subjects who confuse introspection with redemption and irony with understanding. A Marxist who once believed in history's redemptive logic, El-Daif turns to fiction not to overcome failure but to narrate it. In his hands, the novel becomes a space where defeat might be contemplated, cataloged, and restaged. Self-deprecating, digressive, often embarrassingly confessional, his narrative stance enacts a theater of disillusionment in which intellectuals confront their tragedy not through solemnity but through irony and self-parody.

Fractured yet deliberate, earnest yet ironic, nostalgic yet ruthless, El-Daif's prose echoes the broken syntax of the contemporary Arab intellectual's predicament after faith in progress has waned. His characters are the weary heirs of reform: educated, ironic, ambivalent, forever negotiating the distance between admiration and despair. Suspended between collapsing orders, they articulate the exhaustion of a figure once entrusted with moral and historical authority, one that is now reduced, in El-Daif's imagination, to a self-conscious parody of its former gravitas. In his work, modernity is not a horizon to be reached, but a condition to be endured, though not without irony.

*Paving the Sea* (2011) both extends and interrogates El-Daif's lifelong engagement with the Nahda project. The novel functions as a philosophical prequel to his earlier explorations of translation, imitation, and the crisis of modern subjectivity in *Dear Mr. Kawabata* (1995; Eng. 1999) and *Learning English* (1998; Eng. 2013). If translating the modern engenders loss, El-Daif fleshes out in *Who's Afraid of Meryl Streep* (2001; Eng. 2014) a moment of regression to the premodern, to the state of primordial attachments invoking the family, the tribe, the church, the patriarchy.

Where those foundational novels depict late twentieth-century intellectuals confronting the humiliations of linguistic and cultural dependency, *Paving the Sea* returns to origins: to the nineteenth-century Nahda, where the seeds of modern disillusionment were first sown. As he weaves a hybrid narrative that borrows motifs from diverse genres such as historical fiction, biography, and travel literature, all construed at the turn of the nineteenth century, El-Daif reconfigures the historical narratives that imagined and reified modernity.

El-Daif articulates his contemporary ambivalence toward hegemonic historical narratives by displacing Jurji Zaidan's secular, nationalist, and modernist legacy in relation to the paradoxes inherent in the translatability—or impossibility thereof—of the concept of modernity in the Lebanese context. What better way to parody Jurji Zaidan's plight than by building the fictional character Fares Hashem as Zaidan's alter ego, a fictional double on which the narrator projects a wide spectrum of hopes and regrets?

The story of Fares Hashem begins at the intersection of two historical moments that transformed Greater Syria: the civil war of 1860 on the one hand, and the increasingly visible British and French colonial interference in Greater Syria on the other. While Fares aspires to translate Europe's vocabulary of reason into an indigenous idiom of renewal, El-Daif exposes reason as performance: a theater whose gestures reveal the fragility of knowledge rather than its stability. Fares's obsessive pursuit of learning in missionary institutions, his faith in the salvific potential of education, ultimately collapses into absurdity, as rendered in the title of the novel.

Borrowed from a Levantine idiom, to "pave the sea" (*tablīṭ al-baḥr*) is to attempt the impossible: to render the fluid solid, to impose coherence on a world structurally incapable of holding shape. Enlightenment here becomes a labor of futility, a rationality that crumbles under the weight of its own contradictions. The tension between the purposeful and the futile, the push and the pull, the domestic and the wild, the desired and the imposed, is at the center of El-Daif's displacement of the past. The rite of passage to the modern becomes both the quest for the impossible and the rejection of that which is forcefully imposed.

El-Daif's treatment of the Nahda is neither celebratory nor condemnatory. He inhabits its contradictions until they expose themselves, revealing how imitation becomes creation and how the very failure of progress gives rise to a new language of critique. The narrator oscillates between admiration and ridicule, between the desire to emulate Europe and the impulse to mock that very emulation. Fares's adoption of the clichés of Western representation, the mirror through which he perceives himself, becomes a means of exposing their emptiness. The Nahda hero is thus both the embodiment of ideology and the stage of its disintegration, dissection, and mockery.

By exaggerating the orientalist gaze, El-Daif turns it inside out. The reader, suspended between irony and empathy, is compelled to engage in a doubled act of interpretation. The first reading encounters satire that materializes in the grotesque intellectual, the absurd reformer, the farcical dialogue between civilizations. The second reading, slower and more attentive, perceives the critique within the comedy: an interrogation of the very categories through which modernity has understood itself. Irony, in this sense, becomes both method and ethic. It refuses resolution, insisting instead on ambiguity as a mode of truth.

This double structure—what might be termed a "dialectic of parody"—recurs throughout El-Daif's oeuvre. In *How the German Came to His Senses* (2006, Eng. 2015), El-Daif fictionalizes dialogue with the German writer Joachim Helfer; the encounter between Arab and European intellectual traditions becomes a stage for the reenactment of Orientalism under liberal guises. The narrator's feigned innocence, his exaggerated adherence to patriarchal and sexist values, lure his interlocutor into a performance of moral superiority that exposes the persistence of the colonial gaze within modern humanism. The irony of *Paving the Sea* thus extends seamlessly into the global context: The dialogue between Beirut and Berlin repeats, in another register, the comedy of misunderstanding that has haunted the Arab Enlightenment since its inception.

Both texts dramatize the failure of dialogue—precisely, the impossibility of translation—within a world still governed by asymmetries of knowledge and power. The sea, unpaved and infinite, stands as the figure of this refusal: Every attempt at mastery dissolves into motion, every certainty into doubt. Thus, El-Daif writes from within the ruins of ideology, and yet his irony corrodes even the possibility of redemption. His laughter is not cathartic but corrosive, eroding object and subject alike until only the act of exposure remains.

This vulnerability is what gives *Paving the Sea* its distinct texture. El-Daif does not mock the Nahda; he mourns it. His prose parodies its exhausted language without denying its splendor. The novel constructs what might be called a "poetics of aftermath," one that continues to speak in the language of reform while knowing that history has moved elsewhere. Rather than resolving the contradictions of enlightenment, El-Daif allows them to resonate, transforming failure into reflection. Fares's journey becomes that of a thinker who confuses learning with salvation, who believes that knowledge will heal what time has undone, and who discovers, at last, that education is another name for repetition. The more he learns, the less he understands. His search for meaning becomes ritual, his curiosity an act of survival.

Read in this light, *Paving the Sea* imagines the first moment of fascination with Europe, the initial translation of progress into the idiom of reform. Fares's predicament is not personal but civilizational. He embodies the modern subject who inherits two genealogies, one of reason and one of faith, and finds himself unable to reconcile them. His failure is not his alone; it is the failure of a modern subject that cannot locate itself except in mimicry of the other.

El-Daif's achievement lies in turning irony into a form of compassion, in making disillusionment feel like understanding. His prose does not lament the loss of ideals; it listens to their afterlife. To read him is to enter a world in which knowledge has lost its innocence but not its desire, where thinking continues out of habit, longing, and the stubborn will to imagine that meaning, however fragile, still matters. *Paving the Sea* thus emerges as both elegy and affirmation: an elegy for an enlightenment that never fully arrived and an affirmation of the mind's enduring impulse to search, question, and hope.

If El-Daif offers no consolation, he offers lucid disillusionment. His writing dwells in the fatigue of the Nahda rather than its triumph, yet within this fatigue lies a persistent, if fragile, hope embodied in the act of questioning itself. *Paving the Sea* asks what remains of reason when belief in reason has collapsed, what remains of intellectuals when their authority has disintegrated into irony. The answer, if it exists, resides in persistence: in the gesture of narrating, of doubting, of translating again, and laughing throughout.

El-Daif's original prose is haunted by the rhythms of French and English, the grandiloquent patriotic idiom of Nahda litterateurs, and the sober, pained, saccadic prose of mid-century intellectuals. As it demonstrates a spectrum of linguistic sensibility, El-Daif's narrative language performs the layered contradictions of modern Arab consciousness. *Paving the Sea* evokes such layered consciousness: to oscillate between fidelity and betrayal, to risk reproducing the gestures of imitation it critiques. Yet this risk is productive, for it reveals the universality of El-Daif's insight: that modernity itself is a form of mistranslation, a continuous negotiation between origin and echo.

Nicholas R. Lobo and Alfred J. Naddaff's translation extends El-Daif's experiment into new linguistic terrain, inviting readers to confront the paradox of translating a writer whose very subject is the untranslatability of experience. And so the translators' task, like Fares Hashem's, is both hopeful and impossible: to pave the sea, knowing it will not hold. Yet it is in this impossibility that El-Daif's work finds its endurance. Writing, for him, is not the pursuit of certainty but the act of remaining with the question.

To translate him is to join in that act, to continue thinking in the wake of failure, to affirm that meaning, even when fragile, still deserves pursuit.

For the English-language reader encountering El-Daif for the first time, *Paving the Sea* offers both a point of entry into his body of work and an invitation into the intellectual landscape it evokes. The novel speaks from within the crisis of the Arab intellectual in the contemporary era, yet its insights reach beyond the regional, articulating a sensibility that belongs to our shared modernity. El-Daif's prose does not seek to instruct but to unsettle, to make the reader inhabit the unease of a world where knowledge no longer guarantees meaning, where thought no longer redeems. It is a world where seas have dried, where pavement has never offered steady ground.

# Note on Transliteration

In rendering Arabic proper names, terms, colloquialisms, and occasional passages of dialogue in Latin characters, we have decided not to employ an academic style of transliteration. Although such schemes more faithfully reflect the pronunciation of words by distinguishing emphatic consonants (s, t, d, dh/z) and long vowels (a, i, u), they run the risk of offering little to readers who do not know Arabic. Conversely, readers who know Arabic will seldom need these diacritics to identify the original word. Still, our scheme employs two marks beyond the standard English alphabet to assist readers of all backgrounds. First, the acute accent (´), as in Spanish, indicates the stressed syllable in a word when there is ambiguity (e.g., the first syllable in *káshshe,* as opposed to the word cachet), to help nonspecialists be able to sound out words. Second, we use the symbol (ʿ) to indicate the letter *ʿayn,* which represents a consonant sound present in many Semitic languages (the voiced pharyngeal fricative) but absent from English and most languages of Europe.

The names of places and characters are given without stress marks (Fares, not *Fáres*; Kamal, not *Kamál*). Historical personages and locations present a special challenge, as documentary sources might use several Romanizations for a single name, which often reflect the influence of foreign languages (e.g., Rashid and Beirut being rendered *Rachid* and *Beyrouth* in Francophone contexts). We follow the generally accepted English-language transliterations, when available, of the names of real-life figures (Wadih El-Safi, not *Wadiʿ al-Safi*; Abdelkader El-Djezairi, not *ʿAbd al-Qadir al-Jazaʾiri*).

# Dramatis Personae

### Historical Figures

**Ibrahim Pasha (1789–1848):** Egyptian general whose father, Muhammad Ali Pasha (r. 1805–48), wrested Egypt from Ottoman control and established a hereditary dynasty. Ibrahim initiated administrative reforms, occupied Syria (1831–40), and launched successful military campaigns as far as Anatolia.

**Isaac Bird (1793–1876):** Early American missionary in Syria; among the first to establish Protestant schools.

**Asaad al-Shidyaq (1798–1830):** Protestant convert persecuted by the Maronite church; Ahmad Fares's brother (see below).

**Nasif al-Yaziji (1800–1871):** Poet, grammarian, and stylist; worked with missionaries at the American printing press in Beirut.

**Eli Smith (1801–1857):** American missionary and orientalist; assisted Van Dyck and Boustani with the translation of the Bible into Arabic.

**Ahmad Fares al-Shidyaq (1802–1887):** Polymath, linguist, satirist, and author of the autobiographical travelogue *Saq 'ala Saq* (Leg over Leg), published in Paris in 1855 and translated into English in 2014 by Humphrey T. Davies. Shidyaq founded one of the largest Arabic presses in Istanbul and published the newspaper *al-Jawa'ib* (Tidings).

**Emir Abdelkader al-Djezairi (1808–1883):** Algerian resistance leader and Sufi mystic. Exiled to Damascus, he famously protected thousands of Christians during the civil violence in Syria in 1860.

**Rüstem Pasha (1810–1885):** Third Ottoman *mutasarrif* (governor) of Mount Lebanon (1868–73), from an Italian Catholic background.

**Asaad Khayyat (1811–1865):** Reformer and translator who rose to wealth and prominence as the British Consul in Jerusalem, and author of *A Voice from Lebanon, with the Life and Travels of Asaad Y. Kayat.*

**Cornelius van Dyck (1818–1895):** American missionary and physician, who spearheaded the Protestant translation of the Bible into Arabic known today as the Smith–Boustani–Van Dyck version.

**Boutros al-Boustani (1819–1883):** Protestant lexicographer, Bible translator, educator (established the National School in Beirut), journalist and founder of the political and literary magazine *al-Jinan* (Gardens), and author of the encyclopedia *Da'irat al-Ma'arif* (Circuit of Knowledge).

**Henry Jessup (1832–1910):** Missionary and chronicler who penned *Fifty-Three Years in Syria*, published posthumously in 1910.

**Edwin Lewis (1839–1907):** American missionary, linguist, and educator at the Syrian Protestant College whose 1882 commencement speech praising Darwin's methods sparked a debate over science, religion, and education.

**William T. van Dyck (1857–1939):** Cornelius's son; Lebanese-born physician and professor who continued his father's pedagogical legacy.

**Jurji Zaidan (1861–1914):** Lebanese novelist, historian, linguist, and purported originator of the term *Nahda*. After settling in Cairo, he founded a press and published the cultural and literary magazine *al-Hilal* (The Crescent), in which he serialized his twenty-three historical novels.

## Fictional Characters

**Fares Hashem:** The novel's protagonist.

**Mansour "Abu Fares" Hashem:** Fares's father.

**Iskandar Haleem:** Mansour's erudite childhood friend from Brasha who converted to Protestantism in secret after studying with American missionaries.

**Naseem "Abu Zakiyya" Hamal:** Fares's grandfather.

**Zakiyya "Imm Fares" Hamal:** Fares's mother.

**Hasna:** Fares's proud, down-to-earth fiancée from his village.

**Saadeddine al-Jebawi:** A Beirut police officer and close friend of Fares, a like-minded reformist.

**Jamil al-Helou:** A third-year medical student and friend of Fares and Jurji.

**Hanna Haddad:** The gullible caretaker of a village graveyard.

**Yorma:** An older Beiruti prostitute who befriends Fares, sharing her tragic past of abuse and exile.

**Bilat:** An Alexandrian prostitute who proudly embraces her work.

**Mr. Elias:** A strict Orthodox schoolteacher who first teaches young Fares and Jurji.

**Dr. Dale:** An American missionary and physician whom Fares helps deliver cholera medication during an outbreak.
**Jibrael Elias Ward:** A Lebanese volunteer in the U.S. Army whom Fares meets in Cuba.
**Sawa:** A Cuban-born woman of Chinese heritage whom Fares meets while serving in the army.
**Flora:** A Lebanese expatriate in Cuba who shelters Sawa like a sister.
**Kamal Manat:** An interpreter at the Port of Beirut.

# PAVING THE SEA

# 1

Fares Hashem's story began before he was born.

So let's start there.

His story opened with the friendship that for fifty years linked his father, Mansour, to his fellow villager Iskandar Haleem in the nineteenth century—before steamships had begun to moor at the Port of Beirut.

This friendship had a decisive impact upon Mansour's life. Iskandar excelled at reading and writing and memorized poetry. He was acquainted with arithmetic, geography, as well as English, and he was conversant with many mysteries of the universe.

Iskandar received his education at a school founded by the first Protestant missionaries in the village of Souk El Gharb. He was a boarding student, returning home to his own village, Brasha, only for holidays and the summer vacations he would spend with his best friend, Mansour.

Iskandar converted to Protestantism, yet he told no one but his friend Mansour, who was not to divulge the secret even though keeping it was no simple task. After all, these missionary arrivals had come from faraway lands to turn the Christians of the East away from their religion.

The missionaries had truly come from a distant country, America, aboard sailing ships prior to the advent of steam power. At the time, that country had just set off to become the greatest in the world in terms of industry, trade, agriculture, war-making, and the various other sciences. They had come from the same America that, in less than half a century, absorbed tens of millions of young foreign workers to meet its economic demands.

They had come from the same America, then, that was officially known as the United States of America, as people would later discover.

When they first started coming to our country—in the early 1820s—people called them "the English" because they spoke English and enjoyed the protection of envoys of Great Britain.

Like giants, they were physically imposing, light-haired with pale, reddened skin, educated people who held advanced degrees in theology, philosophy, and medicine from the greatest and most prestigious American universities.

They were honest, well mannered, and upright in their behavior. Mansour was amazed by their tales—astonished, even . . . if not for the fact that they wished to lead Christians away from their faith.

They excelled at drawing and would sketch people's faces, their figures and clothes, as well as trees, plants, and animals, houses and the things inside them, streets, paths, cities, landscapes, surviving ancient ruins, the rising smoke of distant fires—everything.

They were faithful to their beliefs, never deviating or deterred by any hardship. At first, they sought to preach the Word of God to all the Muslims of the Ottoman Empire and convert them to Protestantism. Yet they collided with the Muslims' attachment to their religion and faced steadfast resistance from the Ottoman authorities.

The empire, however, was rather lenient with the missionaries when it came to evangelizing other Christians, so the Westerners focused on those communities as a prelude to the Christianization of all Muslim Asia later on. Yet the Christians of the region, Orthodox and Maronites alike, refused to open their doors to the missionaries. They banded together against them, vilified and persecuted them, and prevented them from achieving their goals, particularly during the early stages—with the exception of some violent breakthroughs.

The first of these was when Maronite-born Asaad al-Shidyaq converted to Protestantism and openly avowed the faith. He was consequently detained in a monastery in the Kannoubine Valley in northern Lebanon for four years on charges of insanity. There he died in 1832, and the Protestants considered him the first martyr to fall in Greater Syria. Shortly thereafter, his brother Fares, who would become one of the literary giants of the Nahda—the nineteenth-century Arab cultural renaissance—defied the church and converted to Protestantism, before later converting to Islam, taking the name Ahmad Fares al-Shidyaq, then reverting to his birth confession, it is said, at the final stage of his life.[1]

There was some controversy over this, and conflict erupted between Sunni and Maronite clerics as to where he ought to be buried. So he was not laid to rest in a Muslim graveyard, nor in a Christian cemetery, but among the graves of the *mutasarrifs*—the Ottoman provincial governors who ruled Mount Lebanon—in the Hazmieh neighborhood overlooking Beirut.

There were also breaches among the Orthodox, who would subsequently grow a bit more open to the evangelists.

This hostility and the incidents it caused magnified Mansour's sense of how dangerous the secret he was keeping might be. But to betray a friendship was as difficult as to betray one's religious community. For this reason, he decided to help set fire to the tent that Lyons the missionary had pitched in the outskirts of Brasha, as if to compensate for having kept secret that a native of his village and his denomination had turned to the foreigners' creed.

One day, the people of Brasha learned that Lyons the missionary, on horseback and accompanied by a servant and a guide, had reached the Arayesh Overlook in the village outskirts. There, he pitched a tent, furnished it with rugs and strange things, and took some Protestant books out of a wooden trunk. Meanwhile, the young men gathered in the village square and set out for the overlook. Determined to expel this "Englishman," who didn't believe in the Virgin Mary, from the vicinity of their village, they resolved to set fire to his tent and all its sullied contents.

Leading the charge was Mansour who, by way of Iskandar, knew that this foreign missionary was not an Englishman. He was from a country known as the United States of America: an American. When they first arrived, they encircled the tent, amazed by the fabric it was made from—how

1. The term *nahda*, meaning "revival" or "awakening" (from the verb *nahada*: to stand up or set off), was popularized by the writer Jurji Zaidan (1861–1914), who used it to distinguish the nineteenth-century renewal from earlier periods of literary and cultural flourishing in Arabo-Islamic history, such as from the eighth to eleventh centuries CE at the zenith of the Abbasid caliphs of Baghdad.

new it was, how bright its colors, how prominent its lines and corners. After pausing briefly, they barged into the tent without asking permission and began knocking things over. Some of them even dared to lie down on the same bed on which sat the missionary Lyons, who was baffled as to how he ought to fend off this attack.

Mansour didn't enter the tent, lest the missionary see him and inform Iskandar of his description. He did, however, try to set the tent on fire from the outside with his flint lighter, the way fires were lit in those days. Though the tent failed to catch fire, the smell of what little smoke was produced reached Lyons, who hurried outside to find out what was happening.

Mansour fled to keep the missionary from getting a look at his face.

Once Lyons was sure nothing untoward was going on, he went back inside, having recalled a brilliant ruse.

The boys were still messing around with the things inside the tent, including copies of Protestant liturgical texts, when Lyons made his way through them to grab the sketchbook he used for drawing. He picked it up, took a seat in a corner of the tent, and started sketching them. One of them approached to snatch the sketchbook, but as soon as the boy saw the likeness of his face on the page, he recoiled!

Lyons was aware that people here believed that when a person is drawn on a piece of paper, that person will die the instant the paper is burned, no matter where or when. For instance, if the missionary returned to America and he or someone else set this page alight—even fifty years later!—the person depicted would drop dead at that exact moment, right here in Mount Lebanon. Lyons learned of this belief when sketching a gateway in Beirut's city wall one day. This was years before the cannons of English warships bombarded Beirut in 1840, collapsing the wall and forcing Ibrahim Pasha's forces to retreat to Egypt. At that time, both Egypt and Britain threatened to bring the Ottoman Empire to the brink of ruin.

The missionary was seated, drawing, when a young man snuck up behind him to have a look at the drawing, in which he recognized the gate itself and people and livestock passing back and forth. The boy walked over and stood in the gateway for a while, and when he came back to have another glance at from behind the missionary's back, he saw himself on the page, standing there in the gateway—a perfect likeness. Simultaneously terrified and astonished, he began to sprint through the markets of the city, screaming that Judgment Day had come.

People began following him, and he led them back to Lyons, who was startled that a crowd had gathered around him. They explained to him that drawing is forbidden, that anyone whose likeness is drawn on a piece of paper will die should that page ever catch fire.

The missionary asked them what was to be done.

"Tear it up!" they urged him. He did as he was told, in front of them, and the crisis was peacefully averted.

In this way, when one of the young men in Brasha approached Lyons and glimpsed his own face on the page, he drew back and exited the tent, calling all his companions to come with him, then told them what he saw.

# 2

Mansour was unsettled. In that moment he wished he were able to ask Iskandar for his interpretation.

Upon consideration, they all agreed to ask the servant to convey to the missionary that they would like him to rip up the sketch and refrain from drawing any of them. In exchange, they'd leave him to do as he pleased and provide him with as much bread, eggs, milk, butter, and oil as he wanted, as well as the barley he needed for his mare.

Lyons accepted, on the condition that they pick up the copies of religious texts they'd strewn around, especially the bibles, and return them with care to their places.

Lyons was taken aback by the power of this superstition and its ubiquity among Christians and Muslims alike. Yet Mansour later discovered that this belief was actually a *khuráfa*—a superstition: something counterfactual, a product of the imagination. It was his friend Iskandar who had informed him, explaining what a superstition is and how people in our country believe them because they're ignorant and impious. That was the first time he heard the word *khuráfa*—or its plural, *khurafát.*

"Is life just a bunch of superstitions, then?"

"Yes!" answered Iskandar.

He always believed what his friend told him and took his advice to heart—except when it came to leaving his religion for Protestantism, or abandoning his devotion to the Blessed Virgin Mary and the power of her intercession with God.

Iskandar sent shock waves through the core of Mansour's being, blasting to pieces all his convictions and preconceptions about the world. Iskandar informed Mansour that the Earth is a sphere floating through outer space, revolving around its axis and orbiting the sun, that the universe is infinitely large and home to an uncountable number of stars, that the sky is neither above nor below us, that God does not reside between the stars.

He told Mansour that two-thirds of the Earth's surface is underwater, and land accounts for the last third. He explained that there are five continents in the world, that the two Americas are one single landmass, and that the United States of America is a country located in the northern section of that landmass. He knew a lot about many other countries.

Iskandar apprised him of various discoveries and inventions, of ships propelled by steam power that haul mountains of goods at much higher speeds than traditional ships, about the trains that effortlessly cut across fields and deserts, loaded up with enough people and goods to populate entire cities. He told him about Paris, London, and New York, cities whose buildings house people of different classes, where as many people live in a single building as reside in multiple towns in Greater Syria.

Advancements in the medical field, however, Mansour came to know on his own! Once, Iskandar returned to Brasha when Mansour had fallen ill with tonsillitis. This happened to him periodically, particularly in the springtime. His mother used to ask a healer woman for help, in exchange for two eggs. This healer woman would seek out a girl, necessarily a virgin, who was younger than the patient. Mansour was instructed to lie on his back on the ground, then to cover his eyes and not open them at all. The girl would then stand directly above him so that he was between her legs, her face directly opposite his, and inhale forcefully as the healer pulled a hot iron rod out of the burning embers and submerged it immediately in cold water, producing a distinct noise as the supine patient kept his eyes closed. The girl, standing above him with legs apart, studied his eyes to make sure he did not open them, which would render the operation useless. Another requirement for the cure to work was that the patient not lay eyes on the girl at any point from the moment of her arrival until her departure. The young woman would be compensated in some way for her services.

But the procedure never worked, and Mansour remained in pain for long days at a time. Though he received promises, they proved useless.

No sooner had Iskandar learned of his friend's condition than he hired a mule and returned to Souk El Gharb right away, where the Protestant missionary Dr. Cornelius van Dyck was paying a visit to the school. Iskandar asked for his help, and Dr. van Dyck accepted, accompanying him to Brasha. There, the doctor examined Mansour and prepared him a precise dosage of a medicine carrying a penetrating odor. Mansour took a drink of the medicine and was cured: He sensed an improvement within mere hours of the first dose, and by the next day he'd begun to recover!

By the time Mansour had fully returned to health and regained his spirits, he was distraught. He thought that, to repay Dr. van Dyck for his services, he would have to convert to Protestantism. He shared his concerns with Iskandar, who reassured him that conversion was never expected in exchange for a service—no matter how significant. Conversion happens after arriving at a deep conviction that Christ alone is the savior; that the images and statues in churches are a form of idolatry; that no saint, not even the Virgin Mary, can intercede on a person's behalf with God; and that the only thing that determines one's lot in the hereafter is one's actions in this life.

"I'd sooner die than deny the Virgin Mary's power to intercede," he admitted to Iskandar, "or her holiness."

"You aren't yet qualified to convert to Protestantism," replied Iskandar, "and nobody can force you to do so."

"Then how should I repay Dr. van Dyck for his favor?"

"The doctor doesn't want anything in return. He did it to please the Lord, out of his sense of morality and his conviction that all people are God's children and accountable for one another."

This incident was an especially decisive turning point for Mansour, whose life would become entirely different than it was before.

Modern medicine had enchanted him by the time of his recovery, from an illness that once confined him to bed for days on end each time. No longer was he afraid of it, since the remedy was readily available and could be prepared easily by any doctor within minutes.

He hoped to attend school and become a doctor. But he was the eldest of the family and, after his father's death, its breadwinner. He had six sisters and two younger brothers, so there was no way he could leave work as head mason. Besides, his village Brasha had no school. Anybody wishing to pursue an education had to go to Souk El Gharb, the nearest village with a school—which, despite being well-known for its high caliber, preached the Protestant creed!

When Mansour realized he could never be like his friend Iskandar—God forgive him!—he resolved to achieve his dream through his son, after getting married and being blessed with a baby boy who would study medicine in the modern way. He decided to get engaged, not in the traditional way but by himself, as Iskandar had convinced him, and without entrusting a family member with making the arrangements.

So, on Iskandar's encouragement, Mansour headed off by himself to see Naseem Hamal and ask for the hand of his eldest daughter, Zakiyya, in marriage.

Naseem was astonished by this young man's strange approach, which was contrary to our customs and only practiced, as he'd heard, by suitors in foreign countries. How could this young man show up alone, without sending his parents first? Besides, Naseem, who was decently well-off, dreamt of marrying his daughter to a wealthy man who could read and write, because his daughter was beautiful and quick-witted: a true housewife, with all the characteristics any man could hope for in a wife.

As a result, he declined the request without hesitation and, contrary to the customs of the time, without justifying his refusal with some argument or motive.

"Don't you have a family?" he asked Mansour with disdain.

Mansour departed Naseem's place drenched in the sweat of misfortune and embarrassment, as he described it to his friend Iskandar, whom he went to see the next morning back in Souk El Gharb—eight hours' journey on foot—then asked to meet to tell him what happened and ask his advice. But Iskandar asked him to wait a few weeks until the Christmas holiday when he would return to the village, so Mansour gave him until then, unable to do anything else.

The day after his arrival at the beginning of the Christmas holiday, Iskandar set out alone for the home of Naseem Hamal, who was impressed by the youth's personality and by his gravitas, worldliness, manners, and civility, though he found him to be vastly unlike his age-peers in the village. Naseem only saw him at church on joyous and somber occasions, unaware that Iskandar had left his faith and converted to Protestantism, the religion of the English foreigners.

Iskandar managed to convince Naseem to marry his daughter to Mansour Hashem, and it was the way in which he persuaded him that was remarkable.

"If you marry your daughter to Mansour," he said, "you will be an exemplar of liberation and enlightenment for all of Mount Lebanon, Palestine, Jordan, and Iraq, the whole Arabian Peninsula, the Arab Maghreb—and even Egypt! Throughout the entire Sultanate, in fact.

"You will be the man who married his daughter to a suitor who proposed to her on his own, without entrusting his parents with the matter, in the manner of the foreigners that come to us from sophisticated Europe.

"And, in so doing, you will complete the course charted by the enlightened Asaad Khayyat, the translator who amassed riches and became the British Consul in Jerusalem, then decided in 1835, about a quarter-century ago, to marry in a way consistent with the times, not according to the dictates of threadbare customs.

"Instead, Asaad made a visit to his friend Mr. Habib Jammel who was older than him and something of a freethinker. He was a gentle soul who, when the time for hospitality came, allowed his eldest daughter to serve the guest coffee by herself.

"Asaad's heart jumped when he saw her, face exposed and only her hair covered. The cup nearly fell out of his hand."

But Iskandar had told Naseem a half-truth. Asaad Khayyat indeed chose his own fiancée, but he sent his father to ask for her hand. He'd already gone on his own to see her, having heard good things about her that were favorable to his whims and his modern, liberated ways of thinking. He didn't send his mother, sister, or a female relative to have a look and describe her to him, as was typical. But he did send his father to ask hers for her hand—he didn't dare do so himself.

Asaad Khayyat was a *Nahdawi*: an Arab renaissance man who dreamt that his country would one day rid itself of its backwardness and ascend to the ranks of the European states. Hence, he opposed ignorance, called for women's liberation, and advocated for the intermingling of men and women in public places, and it was in this way he surprised everyone at his wedding by making his wife stand next to him to greet the wedding guests, men and women alike. From as far into the past as people could recall, the custom was that the bride greeted the women and the groom greeted the men, in two separate places.

This was the first incident of its kind in all Greater Syria, and perhaps in all the provinces of the Ottoman Empire.[1] No one could recall a gathering of this sort having occurred before on a similar occasion. Asaad was very proud to have set this precedent, of which he spoke in his memoirs.

Iskandar admired Asaad Khayyat to a great extent and kept up with news of the latter's exploits, which traveled quickly, wherever he could. He, too, was an eager *Nahdawi* who believed in the necessity of emancipating and educating women to become mothers—bearing the great minds who will lead the nation forward on the paths of struggle, who will plant their flags atop the summits of glory.

1. Greater Syria (Arabic: *bilád al-shám*), also known as the Levant or Syria-Palestine, refers to the historical region of the Eastern Mediterranean comprising present-day Syria, Lebanon, Palestine, Jordan, and parts of southern Turkey. Before the establishment of modern nation-states in the twentieth century, the region's inhabitants were broadly called "Syrians," a label not tied to a single ethnicity, confession, or nationality.

# 3

"The mother is the nation!"

This was Iskandar's slogan and that of his like-minded peers, who had begun to grow in numbers at that time.

What Iskandar said was the truth to Mansour who, following Iskandar's instructions, returned to Naseem Hamal by himself and asked his daughter Zakiyya's hand in marriage. The father didn't directly respond to his question and instead called for his daughter. He asked her to serve him some coffee and sit with them, so she took a seat, though on the very edge of the chair and with unbearable timidity. Then her father turned to her.

"Zakiyya, this is Mansour, the mason," he said. "He's here to ask your hand in marriage, by himself—as foreigners do. He chose not to entrust the matter to a parent or relative, tossing aside traditions and customs he calls 'outdated.' So, do you agree to marry him?"

"I shall do as the Lord wills and as you advise, Father!"

"Well, congratulations, then!" Naseem proclaimed to the newly engaged.

He and the groom agreed to complete the engagement soon and that they be married in the coming fall, in roughly a year's time, by which Mansour would be adequately prepared to provide for Zakiyya.

Yet the unfolding of events in Mount Lebanon and Damascus prevented Mansour and his fiancée from carrying out their plan as intended. Several months after celebrating their engagement, the war between the Christians and the Druze erupted in Mount Lebanon, then extended to Damascus.[1]

1. The Druze are a religious community residing mainly in the mountainous regions of Greater Syria. Their faith is based on an esoteric doctrine developed in the early eleventh century out of the Ismaili Shiism of the Fatimid Caliphate.

It is only with great contrition that Lebanese and Syrians from all sects speak of the battles and massacres that took place in Mount Lebanon and the city of Damascus.

The violence claimed the lives of thousands of people, the vast majority of whom were Christians, razed entire villages, towns, and fruit orchards, and forced tens of thousands more to migrate. It remained etched into souls for decades, and perhaps it still is. Among other things, it led to the creation of the Mutasarrifate regime by which Mount Lebanon received its independence from the Ottoman Empire: a preliminary step toward the emergence of the Lebanese nation-state.[2]

Those events were excruciating to an unimaginable extent. People are content to ascribe the conflict to the fact that the Ottomans and English were behind the Druze extremists and the French were behind the Christian extremists and to acknowledge that the events resulted in impossibly heinous bloodbaths.

Seven thousand people, killed within a night and the following day in Damascus! Thousands more, over the course of a few months, were slaughtered in the small villages and towns of beautiful Mount Lebanon—dreamy Mount Lebanon that enchanted prophets and invaders, shepherds, hermits, and passersby throughout the ages, the Lebanon of snow-topped summits and hills in the embrace of springtime.

What a shame!

At any rate, Mansour Hashem's considerations were overturned: The events of 1860 erupted, in all their monstrosity. He and all his fellow villagers were forced to evacuate their homes and seek refuge in Beirut, where several organizations were providing minimal care to the evacuees, estimated to number more than twenty thousand, and where European consuls, missionaries, and foreign merchants wielded the power to influence the Ottoman Empire toward protecting the displaced.

On the way with just a few kilometers until Beirut, however, highwaymen took them by surprise. They attacked and killed several of them,

2. The Mutasarrifate of Mount Lebanon (1861–1918) was a semiautonomous Ottoman district governed by a non-Lebanese Christian administrator (*mutasárrif*), appointed directly by the sultan. This arrangement granted Mount Lebanon limited self-rule within the empire.

making off with anything light enough to carry and of sufficient value. Among the victims was Naseem Hamel, Zakiyya's father.

The day after the fallen were hastily buried in a field near the site of the massacre, Zakiyya's mother approached Mansour.

"If you want my daughter," she told him bluntly, "take her now and look after her yourself. As you can see, everything is falling apart. Otherwise, leave her to me, and the Lord will take care of us just as He takes care of this world."

"I'll marry her now," Mansour replied immediately, and that was that. The village priest who had evacuated with them was summoned, and they were married on the roadside the day after her father's murder.

The first time Mansour had the chance to be alone with his new wife (much to her chagrin) was the night they reached Beirut. Like everyone else from their village, they were sheltered in a schoolhouse close to the American University of Beirut, which was known at that time as the Syrian Protestant College. The school belonged to a Protestant mission from America—one of those that provided relief to at least twenty thousand displaced people from Mount Lebanon and Damascus.

Mansour consummated the marriage with Zakiyya that night in the room they were staying in, which housed both their immediate families and some relatives. At once sly and brutish, he chose a corner for them to sleep and placed Zakiyya between himself and the wall. Her mother lay down behind the wall and fell asleep immediately, out of exhaustion as well as her desire to give the new groom space to take the initiative and, following the nuptial Mass, to finalize the union.

Zakiyya thrashed her arms and legs at the moment of entry. She nearly screamed, were it not for the shame that would have resulted.

Then she cried.

In the morning, she rose and washed the blood from her clothes as she wept, despite having no way to compare what had just happened to her with what she'd dreamt of prior to her marriage. Nine months later, their eldest son, Fares, was born.

Mansour and his wife settled in Beirut permanently, instead of returning to his village, as did his siblings, once things calmed down. It helped that he quickly found a job as a mason with the French company under contract to build the Beirut-Damascus Road, which was to become accessible to horse carriages of all sizes.

Fares was born in a house close to the one in which Jurji Zaidan was born, and on the very same day: December 14, 1861. The two boys grew up as close friends.

The way Mansour Hashem got married bore great resemblance to the marriage of Jurji Zaidan's father, Habib.

The Jurji Zaidan we're talking about is the very same Jurji Zaidan every Arab knows: one of the great pioneers of the Nahda. In his diaries, he spoke about the day he was born in 1861 and how his father was married in 1860. He narrated that this marriage took place the same year as the "notorious unrest," as he called it. The people of Beirut had already grown concerned that the massacres would reach the city, that what happened in Mount Lebanon and Damascus would happen there. They readied themselves to flee.

"The city's in danger," his grandmother told his father at the time, "and, as you can see, we're very worried. So, either marry our daughter immediately and look after her yourself, or we'll break off the engagement and take her with us."

He chose marriage.

The incidents came to an end without Beirut incurring significant damage. People went back to work, and Habib Zaidan returned to managing his restaurant. Then his children were born, the first of whom was Jurji—who, until returning to Beirut the year he got married from Cairo, where he lived at the time, was unaware of his date of birth.

Jurji asked the priest, who had come to welcome him home, about his birthday. The priest replied that they had no records or registers in the church, much to Jurji's disappointment.

His father, who was present, asked his son what was troubling him.

When Jurji told him, he replied: "No one will forget the day you were born, because it was the same day the queen of England's husband died—Prince Albert."

To Habib, it was an unforgettable day because on that very night, while staying up with his friends, he suddenly heard cannon fire coming from the direction of the sea, from the English warships that usually moored there. They grew frightened and considered fleeing the city for the surrounding mountains, concluding that these ships were firing on the city. Later, they learned that it was on account of the death of the queen's husband.

"You were born the same day the Queen of England's husband, Prince Albert, died: the fourteenth of December, 1861."

It was raining the day Fares and Jurji were born. It had been raining steadily for roughly ten days, following months of drought during which a contagious disease began to spread. People called it "breakbone fever"—or *Ábu Rékab* in Arabic, "the knee thing," because it caused sharp pain in the knees.

The outbreak appears to have resulted from waste left behind by twenty thousand people displaced by the sectarian massacres from their villages in Mount Lebanon, Damascus, and the surrounding areas.

For eleven months, twenty thousand immigrants took up makeshift residence in a city of forty or fifty thousand, and without modern infrastructure! Back then, drinking water had yet to be drawn from Dbayeh down into Beirut. Microbes multiplied rapidly, and the drought contributed to the spread of these germs and diseases.

At the time, Mansour and Habib were worried about their wives catching this disease, so they made plans to send them both to their relatives in a Mount Lebanon village outside Beirut. But, in the end, it began to rain before they could carry out their decision. The downpour came after people had become fearful and desperate, after they prayed repeatedly for rain. Fuad Pasha, the Ottoman governor of Beirut, invited the whole community to attend a joint rain prayer held by Muslim and Christian holy men. So strong was the faith of several clerics leading the gathering in the sincerity of their prayer that they were holding umbrellas!

"Whosoever has a single grain of faith," one of the Christian clerics proclaimed, addressing the crowd with an umbrella in hand, "may command the mountains to move, and they will move!"[3]

3. This recalls Matthew 17:20: "If you have faith as a mustard seed, you will say to this mountain, 'Move from here to there,' and it will move; and nothing will be impossible for you." (New King James Version).

A Sunni cleric gave a sermon to the same effect.

The gathering hadn't yet concluded when the winds blew in, thunder rolled, and rain began to pour down!

It was a miracle!

# 4

That was a perturbing day for Mansour Hashem. He attended the prayer with his friend Habib solely out of curiosity.

He was unconvinced that God would have answered the call of those clerics, whose faith, after all, Iskandar had advised him not to trust. He tried to come up with a logical explanation for what had happened and supposed that before inviting people to the ceremony, Fuad Pasha had seen the dark clouds growing and sensed the impending rain. But Mansour was himself skeptical of this explanation, influenced by his friend Iskandar's theory to the effect that God, who created the universe and set it in motion, does not get involved in minutiae and tends to leave people to manage their own affairs.

Habib, Jurji's father, was in a hurry to get to his restaurant, which he had left in the care of a young man in his employ.

The day after Fares and Jurji were born, the weather was still rainy—and construction workers don't work on rainy days. Mansour went to see Habib at his restaurant to help him as he usually did on his days off. He arrived soaked in rainwater and found two blond foreigners inside. He recognized one of them immediately: Dr. Cornelius van Dyck, who had cured him from his sickness. He would later learn that the second was the Protestant missionary Henry Jessup.

Accompanying them was the teacher Boutros al-Boustani, who was discussing the translation of the Old Testament into Arabic with van Dyck. Henry Jessup mostly listened. The three of them spoke Arabic at times and English at others, and, after speaking at length about the Torah translation, they moved on to the topic of the school Boustani resolved to establish in the wake of the previous year's massacres. He wanted to found a "national" school for the very first time in the history of the whole country.

In doing so, he sought to combat ignorance by propagating knowledge, to thwart sectarian fanaticism by promoting an inclusive patriotic ethos, and to confront fear of the Other by habituating people of different sects to intermingle and engage with one another. After all, ignorance of the Other drives people to hostility. At length they discussed the matter of whether people would accept such a notion, whether they would send their children to a place where they would not learn the teachings of their religion. Boustani's opinion was that the school shouldn't teach religion. Instead, parents would be allowed to choose their own holy man, and the school would handle taking the students to him for lessons and then bringing them back.

Mansour was unsettled to hear what he heard, as he confided in Abu Jurji. His friend told him that he would enroll Jurji in that school once his son reached the right age, provided he managed to afford the fees. Mansour responded excitedly that he, too, would send his son to this school when the chance presented itself.

He decided to take the first opportunity to tell this to Iskandar, who had already written to say he was coming to visit Mansour over the Christmas holiday to congratulate him on the birth of his son Fares, "may the Lord grant him a long life in service of truth and the nation!"

Fares's mother didn't understand this remark. Wishes are made for a long life devoted to family and faith, not one spent in service of the so-called *wátan*—the homeland: that word she'd started hearing educated men use in their conversations. A long lifetime ought to be spent in service of religion above all. At the time, it was impossible to imagine the world outside of religious terms. The word "nation" in the modern European sense was only in use among the small elite who had come under the influence of European modernism.

After Boustani and the two missionaries left, Habib "Abu Jurji" Zaidan informed Mansour Hashem that he had been too embarrassed to express his joy over the birth of the latter's son in the presence of those two foreigners, lest they assume that the reason for his great excitement was that the newborn was a boy, not a girl, then mock him in the way foreigners usually mocked the people of our country who hated for their wives to bear girls . . . [1]

These Western men, who sat to eat at tables in lofty chairs and used spoons and forks and knives, who wore trousers and put European-style hats on their heads instead of fezzes, making fun of our preference for boys over girls! Worst of all, they shaved their mustaches to the point of resembling women.

(Fares came running to his father once, panting and shaken up:

"*Bába*! *Bába*!" he called. "I saw a man with no mustache!"

"Where?!" his father asked—

. . . and ran after the boy to see for himself.)

When Fares and Jurji were born, the missionary Jessup gave a copy of the Gospels in his new translation to each of the boys' fathers. Abu Jurji thanked him and, in exchange for this gift, invited Jessup to have lunch at his restaurant for free. Jessup accepted the invitation.

"I acquiesce in your serving me lunch in exchange for this gift. It's as if you've paid its price this way," he remarked, then continued: "And I welcome those who pay the price of the Gospel. To obtain it is well worth the trouble."

Abu Jurji surely took Jessup's point, but Mansour understood better what the "English" missionary was getting at. His friend Iskandar used to tell him about Protestant doctrine in detail and at length, so he was aware of the Bible's symbolism to Jessup: In it, pure souls shall find the indisputable Truth!

Mansour would always meet Jessup there and talk to him without worrying about being convinced by what he had to say, because he felt as if he were inoculated against these teachings, with which he was now quite familiar. Jessup liked Mansour and admired his dedication to his work

1. In Arabic, a *kúnya* is a standard honorific by which a person is referred to by the name of their first-born child (or eldest son), prefixed with "father of" or "mother of." The forms used in the Levant are *ábu* and *ímm*, respectively. Hence, Habib Zaidan is called *Abu Jurji* just as Mansour Hashem and Zakiyya Hamal are called *Abu Fares* and *Imm Fares*.

and his devotion to providing for his wife and son and helping his mother, brothers, and sisters—without grumbling or expecting thanks.

Once, Jessup made him a promise to sponsor his son Fares's education at one of the missionary schools when he turned six years old. Mansour smiled without saying anything about the promise. But van Dyck, who was present, understood the meaning of that smile.

"Fear not," he reassured Mansour, in a mixture of literary and vernacular Arabic. "We'll not turn him away from his religion by force!"

But Mansour was unconvinced, for anything that can be taken by force can also be won with kindness. He wasn't educated, but he did love knowledge and to be in the company of the learned.

He was enchanted by what Mr. Boutros al-Boustani and Dr. Cornelius van Dyck had to say any time he encountered them at Abu Jurji's restaurant and overheard them discussing highly important matters. Sometimes these were dangerous notions, like forming a secret society that works internally and externally to separate Syria—today's Lebanon, Syria, and Palestine—from the Ottoman Empire and establishing a nation-state where all people are equal before the law. It would have no fixed religion; rather, its constitution would be inspired by the fundamental common principles of all Abrahamic religions. The state would leave freedom of belief and worship to the people: to each their faith as they saw fit.

# 5

Mr. Boutros al-Boustani and Dr. Cornelius van Dyck also spoke about the idea of establishing an institute of higher learning where local students could study medicine (in the Western sense of the word). They would discuss the paramount importance of this school for the rebirth and improvement of the countries.

Boustani and Dr. van Dyck paid no mind to the fact that Mansour could hear their conversation and that he understood what they were saying. They even thought he was some uneducated, mountain-dwelling oaf with a petrified mind—inflexible, stubborn, and unable to grasp subjects like these. But he did understand. And what he understood elicited strong, amorphous emotions within him and further encouraged him to send his son Fares to school when he reached the right age. These conversations increased his dedication to his dream that his son become a doctor.

Mansour felt proud as he imagined his son Fares one day speaking like these two men spoke, and with the same depth.

He sent Fares to school at the age of five, which was young in those days. But he followed the example of Habib, Jurji's father, who wished to begin his son's schooling early. Mansour sent his son to the school where Jurji's teacher, Mr. Elias—the brother of Father Mousa, an Orthodox priest whose congregation included the Zaidan clan—taught, and not to the national school founded by Mr. Boustani, because it was too far away for a boy of five.

Despite his deep Christian faith, Mansour wished he were able to send his son to Mr. Boustani's National School, which was secular, as one would say nowadays. But at that time, learning was still the prerogative of holy men or those associated with them. To send a child to a secular school that would not teach him the principles of his faith was cause for scandal in the neighborhood. And though Mansour was unable to challenge this reality, he didn't want it to prevent him from sending his son to school. After all, he placed great hopes on the boy: It was Fares who would make his father's dream a reality.

But the school where Jurji and Fares were sent wasn't a school in the sense we understand today. It had one teacher, the proprietor, who taught only reading—despite scarcely being able to read himself—and occasionally some principles of arithmetic.

This school consisted of a large cellar with rugs on the ground upon which the students sat opposite the teacher, who sat on a low seat in front of which was a *bishtákhta*—a small box on which to place his book, instruments, and pens—and next to which lay some rods, most of them sugarcane. They were of different sizes and thicknesses, each and every one of which he would use according to how close the student was to him and how serious his offense.

Though Jurji Zaidan never took a "whacking," as they say, Fares did several times. Perhaps it was the sight of his friend, legs raised and bound with a rope and stick as Mr. Elias struck his feet with a rod of pomegranate wood, that kept Jurji well-behaved at all times, lest the same fate befall him.

Perhaps.

Who knows?

Even so, it would fill Jurji with rage to watch the teacher strike his friend so sternly and deliberately.

Fares kept himself from screaming out in pain to frustrate the teacher, to retaliate with his endurance and silence.

Mr. Elias forbade the students from scratching their heads after he gave them the rod. Anyone who violated his orders by scratching their head would get another, harsher beating.

"Don't you scratch!" he'd yell. "You'll recover!"

He believed that if your head is struck with a cane and you don't scratch it, you'd become stronger and tougher than before. When the teacher smacked him on the head with the pole, Fares would usually scratch it intentionally, and out of spite. The teacher lost his temper, as did Fares, on one occasion.

He carried on hitting him, barking at Fares, "Don't scratch, you'll be fine!," as he continued to scratch his head to spite and defy the man until, finally, the cane snapped into pieces against his head and was no longer usable.

The teacher considered reaching for the next rod but abruptly changed his mind and inhaled deeply, filling up his lungs. He was quiet for a moment, then resumed his explanation. Jurji's chest filled with pride for his friend, and all the students felt a sense of victory and vengeance.

The next day, the students entered the cellar to find the teacher holding a cane, uncharacteristically, before the lesson had begun. Yet he didn't strike anyone with it the entire day.

By the end of the two years Jurji and Fares spent with Mr. Elias, the two had "concluded the sciences" and were now "deconstructing the word," as the teacher assured their fathers. They had, in fact, begun reading the Psalms—yet without understanding anything. Later, they were forced to part because Jurji's father sent his son to a school that had recently opened. It was known as the Damascene School, in reference to a group of Orthodox intellectuals from Damascus who founded it after fleeing to Beirut in the wake of the 1860 massacres. That was a prestigious school, employing modern pedagogical methods inspired by the institutions established by Catholic and Protestant missionaries.

Yet this school was closed in 1870: just two years after Jurji enrolled. That day, the faculty instructed parents to send their children to the Greek Orthodox School of the Three Holy Hierarchs, where many renowned teachers had been appointed, and most of the students followed them. This school taught grammar, arithmetic, and French.

Jurji spent another two years here, after which, once again, he had to drop out—having begun to take pleasure in learning and having become enchanted by knowledge. Nothing else mattered to him anymore. No longer was he the least bit inclined to play, unlike all the other students his age. No longer did he fly kites, which were very popular toys, and only rarely did he play with a ball or with marbles. Occasionally he'd come outside to observe the launch of a massive kite that all the neighborhood children would gather to watch, but he did not take part in the game.

Fares, however, went neither to the Damascene School nor the School of the Three Holy Hierarchs, but to a school run by Catholic monks. His father wanted to send him to the national school, but he came under the influence of some monks; that the Catholic school was very close to home had weakened his argument significantly.

This school followed modern methods and curricula, but the monks who taught there were generally strict, which is what very much pleased the parents.

"I entrust my son to you in flesh and bone," Abu Fares told the monks who received his son, "so take the flesh, and leave me the bones!"

By that he meant for them to be ruthless with his son whenever possible, to beat him without pity if he misbehaved, yet without breaking his bones. At the time, bones were understood to be the foundation of the human being; flesh was something secondary, fluid.

In those days, parents liked for the teachers to beat their children severely until they developed good manners and became educated, and it was a pleasure for the teachers to strike the students.

Fares enjoyed playtime much more than school, but he was an avid reader and very intelligent. His wits permitted him to study in moderation and meet the requirements without difficulty, sometimes with honors, but still he regularly faced beatings with thick sticks—worst of all those unbearable pomegranate canes.

If not for his determination to achieve his father's dream, now his own; if not for his intelligence, love of knowledge, and appreciation of the role science was to play in the country's advancement; if not for having integrated into the avant-garde elite—he'd have dropped out of, or been expelled from, school.

Habib Zaidan did not allow his son Jurji to swap his *sirwâl*—loose-fitting, Ottoman-style pants with a drawstring—for European trousers, lest the children of the neighborhood where the restaurant was located make fun of him. Mansour, on the other hand, encouraged Fares to take off the *sirwâl* and wear pants his first day at the new school, but Fares kept his red fez on his head and his Ottoman jacket.

When Jurji saw Fares wearing pants that evening, he couldn't help bursting out in laughter.

Fares told Jurji that he felt as if his legs were weak and incapable of carrying his body when wearing these pants. He bent over, looked at them, and guffawed nearly to the point of fainting.

Later, fate would have it that Jurji was forced to drop out of school at the end of his second year, when he was eleven years old. This was because the waiter—or *sáfarji*, in the language of those days—quit his job and didn't return. There was no way his father could run the restaurant by himself, so he asked his son to help him temporarily until he found another *sáfarji*, or until the previous one changed his mind and came back. His father hoped the latter would happen, as this waiter had grown up in their house.

"Seven or eight days," the father told his son Jurji, "till I find someone to take your place."

His son begrudgingly acquiesced. He'd taken such unimaginable pleasure in learning, and he promised himself he'd go back to school in seven or eight days.

But those days lasted so long that they became seven or eight *years*!

Seven or eight years Jurji Zaidan spent in the markets of Beirut among the masses, during which time he had to associate with all manner of people. Their restaurant was in the middle of the city, and though it changed locations several times, it was never far from Burj Square: a rendezvous point at the time for thugs, riff-raff, and the unemployed.[1] Among them were drunks, gamblers, brothel-keepers, and gangsters—these were the people Jurji was forced to interact with. They were at their liveliest at night, and the prostitution of adolescents was widespread.

Jurji bemoaned the situation he found himself in, while Fares envied him for it. He hated school and would often feign illness, play truant, and seek out Jurji at the restaurant. He would often go in the evening where he had become acquainted with many of those youths—the "procurers and delinquents," as Jurji used to call them—and befriended some of them. Jurji always used to warn him to keep away from them, lest they entangle

1. Known today as Martyrs' Square (*sáhat al-shúhada*), in honor of the Syrian and Lebanese nationalists who were executed there in 1916 by Ottoman governor Djemal Pasha.

him in something undesirable. Yet he simultaneously admired his friend's bravery and recklessness.

During this period, Fares taught Jurji how a man milks himself.

"Do what I'm doing!" Fares told him the first time Jurji masturbated with him. He told Jurji what those youths would do together, which simultaneously elicited his disgust and piqued his curiosity.

At first, Jurji was unable to reach climax. He regretted what he'd done and felt a painful sense of guilt. He prayed to the Virgin Mary, swearing never to do that again.

Once, when he was only twelve years old, Fares went alone down to Whore Alley, where the prostitutes lived and conducted business, and found the courage to knock on one of the doors.

A fleshy woman answered the door, her bosom nearly spilling out of her shirt.

"You hungry, baby?" she mocked. "Want to nurse?"

Then she shut the door in his face.

When he told Jurji, they shared a hearty laugh.

# 6

At that time in 1873, some of Mansour's relatives arrived at Beirut from Brasha, accompanied by a number of other villagers, on their way to America. They planned to charter a ship from the harbor and needed time to complete their business. They had to await the arrival of the ship that would transport them, so they lodged with their relative and fellow villager Mansour Hashem. They stayed about two weeks, during which they convinced him to come with them.

Their argument was irrefutable: Mansour couldn't expect a thing from this poor, unstable country if he wanted to educate his son Fares to become a doctor and realize his dream, and if he wanted to buy a house, to start his own business. If that was truly what he wanted, all he had to do to make his dream a reality was to go with them, stay there for several years working and saving money, then come back.

There, life "couldn't be better"!

There, the land is gold!

Migrating to America hadn't yet become widespread, hadn't yet transformed into an alarming phenomenon that emptied out the villages of Mount Lebanon. That phenomenon would begin its frenetic expansion several years later. Yet Mansour often heard about America from his friend Iskandar and the missionaries he used to encounter at Habib Zaidan's restaurant, so he was swift to make the official arrangements, especially the ticket that at the time served as a passport and was issued by the Ottoman authorities.

Then, he gathered his things—a thin mattress and blanket, a pillow, some supplies, some grain and dried vegetables, and a bottle of *arak* (or *mqásheh*, as it was called in those days)—and put them in a wooden trunk that he carried on his back.[1] He brought it down to the harbor with his relatives and fellow villagers, his whole family accompanying him to bid him farewell.

Fares was both happy and disquieted about saying goodbye to his father at the quay. He was glad because he loved to spend his time as he liked, and his father was very tough on him, always wanting him to be like Jurji: serious, indifferent toward play, and devoted to his ongoing studies. However, Jurji had stopped going to school for almost the past two years. Fares secretly envied him, without having the courage to admit it to his father, or even to himself.

He was happy because his father's departure would lessen his supervision, and because his mother was exceedingly lenient. Mothers are compassionate by nature.

He was uneasy because migrating is somewhat like dying, and his father, as harsh as he was to Fares, was still his father. He didn't want that to happen to him, nor did he want him to be so far away.

Mansour's family didn't hear from him at all for the first four or five years after his departure, because he struggled greatly before reaching New York and settling there. Obstacles stood in his way the moment he set foot in New York Harbor, when the doctor examined him and determined that he was unable to enter the city because he had an infectious disease. All that was actually wrong with him was some yellowing in his complexion from the exhaustion of travel and some redness in his eyes from the ocean sun.

He gathered his strength, counted his money, and asked the relatives he traveled with to lend him some more. He committed their addresses to memory, then recorded them on a piece of paper he hid in a pouch he wore around his neck and that dangled against his chest beneath his clothes. He went to Mexico, with the help of the official interpreter—a native of Mount Lebanon in the employ of the New York Port Authority—who helped him buy a ticket, instead of returning to Beirut crestfallen.

1. *Arak* (also spelled *araq*) is a traditional Levantine distilled spirit made from fermented grapes and flavored with aniseed, similar to the Turkish *rakı* and Greek ouzo.

This interpreter was unable to mediate on behalf of his countryman Mansour. The Port Authority had threatened to fire him several times due to how often he mediated on behalf of immigrants with his background and showed them extralegal ways to escape the harbor and enter New York City. At the time, Ellis Island had yet to be designated for this purpose.

When Mansour arrived at quarantine in Mexico, the interpreter there led him to the immigrants from his region, who welcomed him and took him in for several days to relax. Then they packed him a box of utensils and cookware that had been used by housewives and took him to become a peddler on the skirts of cities where there were no shops. After working as a peddler for about a year and a half and saving some money, he decided to enter the United States by land and reach New York, his primary objective, no matter the cost.

In this way he kept moving from city to city, from state to state, until he finally reached New York after years of wandering—all the while his family heard nothing from him, nor he from them. He didn't want to write to them unless the letter contained the money they needed and was marked with his fixed address.

When no one had heard from the father and, as a result, his family had not received any income for some time, there was no longer any way Fares could continue his education. So, after a time—less than two years—he was forced to drop out. Though he was disappointed, he wasn't terribly upset. He had fallen in love with knowledge and learning, and he was aware of their impact upon his future and their capacity to improve the country, but he could never fully adjust to school. He used to dream of a different way to get an education, or of another school, where the discipline was less severe.

This is how Fares started to spend much of his time in Burj Square, where he'd go from his house at the foot of the hills of Achrafiye, located outside of present-day Beirut. He seldom strayed far from Jurji Zaidan's father's restaurant, so not an hour would pass without him walking by, conversing with Jurji and telling him what had happened to him and what he had seen. Jurji was enchanted by his friend's freedom and his audacity, so, on occasion, he kept Fares company in his wandering—but without allowing the situation to consume him.

During this phase, they practiced the "secret habit" so often that it began to weaken their bodies.

They would sit in deserted places and masturbate, and it would amaze them when the "strength" came out of them. Then they would begin contemplating and exchanging thoughts about it:

"The essence of human strength!"

"The essence of the human spirit!"

"The elixir of life!"

They would gaze at this strength as if it were of metaphysical significance. Or perhaps the embarrassment prompted them to use such "unscientific language," as Fares would later call it.

Fares had just turned thirteen when he had to leave school, and his uncles forced him to work with them in Brasha as a builder. But he didn't remain in this line of work for long, and he'd never imagined spending his life as a mason. His mother, Zakiyya, adored his aspiration to get an education and become a doctor, and she hoped that this dream—his father's dream—would come to fruition. So she wasn't upset when Fares left work with his uncles in construction and stone cutting, nor did she press him to reconsider.

To compel him to stay in the village and keep working for them, his uncles tried to convince him to get engaged to a girl his age named Hasna: the daughter of a villager who used to work with them. From time to time, she would bring her father lunch. She was mature and looked much older than she was, as if she were seventeen. Fares's uncles noticed him glancing at her with desire, so they took advantage of the situation. They planned to ask her father for her hand one afternoon when she brought his lunch. Fares stood firm in his refusal and thwarted their plot.

He actually *did* have a crush on her, though. He would furtively meet her at night in a house evacuated by its residents two years before. Their meetings never went beyond conversation, since she didn't allow him to get close to her and touch her. They were later discovered, and after that it was impossible for him to see her. When he returned to Beirut, he attempted to send her many letters because she knew how to read, albeit with difficulty, but they didn't reach her and came back to him. He had wished to stay in touch with her, then to get married—not in the outmoded, conventional way, and not straightaway, but after realizing his dream to specialize in medicine. Then he tried to forget the matter and gave up, only to subsequently learn that she had left with her parents for America.

It occurred to Jurji that Hasna wasn't some starry-eyed romantic who longed to have her heart broken. She was a practical young woman: When she took a liking to something and couldn't make it a reality, she'd move on to something else she was capable of achieving.

And that was that.

Fares worked with his uncles for only a few months, then returned to Beirut for good. A short time afterward, he managed to find work as a teacher in the city of Zahle after convincing the school administration that he was seventeen, as his appearance clearly suggested.

# 7

Cholera broke out that year. First it beset some villages near the city, especially the town of Habbine, so the Protestant missionaries eagerly applied themselves to serving the people whom the Ottoman authorities had left to their dismal fates. But many hardships stood in their way, most significantly the fact that armed guards from these villages prevented anyone from approaching and entering for fear of infection. Anyone found between one village and the next was a cause for fear, a courier of the seeds of death—and was considered, therefore, fair game to kill.

News of Habbine's cholera outbreak reached Zahle, so the American missionary Dale volunteered to go there with a supply of "Hamlin's" medicine, which he obtained from Beirut. But he couldn't find a donkey driver or anyone to accompany him there—save for Fares, who volunteered to come with him. Dale accepted the offer.

Many people urged them not to go, and some threatened them with not being allowed to return to the city lest they spread the disease.

When they reached the village, they found that many of its people had fled to the surrounding mountains and taken up residence there, including Christian and Muslim clerics who were powerless to do anything. The infected had been left to suffer by themselves, or with parents or relatives brave enough to stay with them.

There were about thirty infected people in the village, only one of whom died. The rest recovered—thanks to Dr. Dale and his local assistant, Fares, as well as the medicine they'd brought. Days later, the church bell rang, the call to prayer sounded from the mosque, and the fearful evacuees returned.

"Knowledge!" exclaimed Fares to himself, recalling his father's ambition.

Dale insisted that Fares accept payment, but Fares insisted on refusing.

Fares was proud of this accomplishment, and he felt an inner calm and near invulnerability. A person's sacrifice for the sake of their impoverished, downtrodden people is an exceedingly noble objective, indeed!

This sacrifice did not, however, keep the director and proprietor of the school from discovering that Fares was younger than he let on. Upon finding out, they then wanted to decrease his pay to children's wages. Fares refused and left the school, after having worked there for about a year.

Three years later of digression, indecision, and anticipation, Fares returned to school—after his mother, Zakiyya, sold every plot of land they had once owned in the village and sold her husband's share in the family home to his brothers.

Before that, Zakiyya used to work as a housemaid and had a knack for spinning woolen sweaters, which she used to sell. She earned more than she needed each day, which allowed her to save up. She was a problem solver. She decided not to send all her children to school, as she couldn't afford it. Fares used to give her some of his earnings when he worked, so this, too, she saved.

Zakiyya was convinced that good news from her husband would soon arrive, even though his absence had grown long, and doubts got the better of her more and more with each day. Many questions disquieted her. How was she to describe her situation: abandoned, divorced, or widowed? Being in limbo was taking a heavy toll on her health and spirits.

Fares returned to school, setting before himself a single goal that he'd decided to accomplish no matter the difficulties he faced: to become a doctor and achieve his personal dream—and that of his father, from whom they no longer heard—and to perform his patriotic duty.

The wandering phase Fares had just exited was neither a waste of his time nor a total removal from the academic atmosphere. He kept abreast of scientific and literary developments in the city and continued to read and prepare himself for the day he would inevitably return to school. He stayed in contact with a number of nationalist professors at the American

University and missionaries that came to Abu Jurji's restaurant, who took notice of Fares's intellect, refinement, and desire to better himself.

At that stage, Fares came to know Saadeddine al-Jabawi, who was older and had just started his tenure with the Beirut Ottoman police. The two formed a lasting friendship. They shared the very same ideals, the very same dreams.

This stage of Fares's youth was very rich in life experiences. It allowed him to mingle with many kinds of people in this transforming city, now home to some sixty thousand residents, having had only forty thousand just a few years before.

Not an opportunity went by during that period without Fares taking part as much as he could. He volunteered to combat the massive waves of locusts that had infested the country, so many of them as to block out the sun. They were landing in valleys, atop mountains, in cities and villages—shrouding them like a bunch of rugs without defined edges. They descended upon Beirut, then annihilated every last tree, blade of grass, piece of fruit, and seed. The authorities encouraged people to take part in exterminating the pests. Fares, along with Jurji, became actively involved in the campaign, and the two worked for several days until late at night, managing to amass a great many bags of locusts.

But one day they were so exhausted they didn't take the bags all the way to the public dump to be destroyed by fire or buried in dirt. Instead, they set them down inside the restaurant with the understanding that they'd come back in the morning to take them to the designated location. But, the next morning, Jurji's father got there first, to be dumbfounded by locusts filling up the street, his shop, and the shops next door. All food and supplies were lost.

That wave of locusts led to the early stages of a famine caused by food shortages and the ensuing price hikes. Thefts increased, as did crimes against people and property, public and private.

Yet Beirut soon overcame that crisis and returned to her beautiful disposition.

Fares didn't let a single event pass him by during that period. He used to implore Jurji to come look at things that, in Jurji's view, were insignificant, like when a new business or workshop opened. What's more, Fares nearly went without him to the celebration in honor of water having been drawn from the Dbayeh region into Beirut. That was in 1875, and it was an unforgettable day. Prominent individuals were in attendance, notably the Emir Abdelkader el-Djezairi, the Ottoman governor of Beirut, and the Mutasarrif of Mount Lebanon. Their friend Saadeddine let them stand close to the rostrum, as he was part of the police squad tasked with maintaining order.

Fares was astonished as he watched the Emir Abdelkader approach from up close, atop his horse, surrounded by a grand procession, then dismount and take his place on the platform.

He couldn't believe his eyes.

There he was: the great national hero, the resistance fighter against the French occupation in Algeria, the wise thinker, the one who protected as many Christians as he could amid the bloodbath of 1860 in Damascus. He was the subject of wide, international acclaim.

Fares looked at Jurji and saw that he, too, was amazed by what he was seeing.

"What do you make of that?" Fares asked.

At this ceremony, Fares felt as if he were taking part in the forging of Beirut's future, and he was proud to do so. Drinking water now flowed to people's homes through metal pipes. Citizens could obtain water with ease, without having to go outside to a faraway well or spring at night in the cold. They could consume as much as they pleased, whenever they pleased. Anyone passing through now had access to pure water from the drinking fountains spread throughout the neighborhoods.

In 1876, Fares spent his days tirelessly going from place to place to see the emperor of Brazil, Pedro II, who had come to visit the Ottoman Empire and spent several days in Beirut. The emperor invited people to immigrate to Brazil to work, and his visit indeed served to inspire a massive wave of migration there.

People grew very fond of the emperor's exploits, his love of Beirut, and his erudition. It was said that he studied Arabic before he arrived, under the tutelage of an expatriate from Mount Lebanon, and that he became proficient during his brief stay in the region. News spread widely that he prayed in Arabic, the language nearest to God. It was the sister language of Hebrew, in which the Jewish prophets received their revelations, and of Aramaic, which the Lord Jesus Christ spoke—and the very tongue by which the Quran was revealed to the Arab Prophet.

# 8

During his stay in Beirut, the emperor visited the American printing press and the American University College of Medicine, both of which impressed him. Fares heard that, while visiting the college, the emperor asked how the cadavers were brought there for the students to take their gross anatomy course. His question attracted the attention of all the professors and students present, as this was a very sensitive issue. Anatomy was a required subject on the final exam in Istanbul, and those who passed were licensed to practice medicine in all the Ottoman lands. He was told that the university would purchase the bodies of the poor who had been put to death and receive others that were unclaimed free of charge.

This information shook Fares to his core.

Where were the bodies coming from?

At Abu Jurji's restaurant, a professor told Fares in confidence that they received, by various means, the bodies of people who had been killed. He gave no more detail than that: He didn't know, nor was he supposed to know. But Fares's friend Saadeddine al-Jabawi, the police officer, told him that the city police were aware that many of these bodies that ended up at the university belonged to women and girls, some of whom had been killed to protect their families' imperiled honor. Others were killed for "unknown" reasons, including those murdered on false accusations of dishonor. Put simply, women were killed so their bodies could be sold.

On several occasions, the college received women's bodies that had been found discarded near Whore Alley. Far more women's bodies were received than men's.

Then Saadeddine told Fares something he urged him not to share: that some high-ranking officials would take their cut for the bodies to reach the dissection hall. They even knew about bodies that were stolen within hours of being buried.

Fares thought to himself that the emperor of Brazil was a well-informed man, and that his question only appeared to be innocent.

In his years of wandering and anticipation, Jurji seldom dared to visit the brothels in Whore Alley—or "behind the barracks," as people used to say. The two or three times he went were at the encouragement of Fares, who had no misgivings about seeking out life's pleasures. At that time, condoms weren't used as widely as they are today, so prostitutes only allowed distinguished, well-educated elites and notables to penetrate them. The others were served with their hand or under the armpit.

But Fares was able to convince one of his favorites, Yorma—who was over fifty—to let him enter her. Once, he even succeeded in bringing her to orgasm, so she lowered the night's price. He began to feel more and more at ease with Yorma. They developed such a strong relationship over time that she told him her life story and revealed her secrets, explaining how she ended up in this degrading profession. This story had a profound impact on Fares's life, igniting a fierce passion to pursue medicine at all costs. It also strengthened his conviction of the need to build a modern, fair, and compassionate country on equal footing with the sophisticated nations of Europe.

Yorma, the eldest daughter, was raped by her father after her mother's death. Then she was raped by her cousin and became pregnant with his child. Or perhaps it was her father's—how could she have known?

When her father noticed her protruding belly, he panicked, as he imagined the scandal it would bring (unaware of what his own nephew had been doing to her). He threatened to kill her unless she left home and rid herself of the demon inside her. She was just thirteen years old at the time.

She contemplated attributing the pregnancy to her cousin. When he initially raped her, he didn't notice blood on either of them and accused her of not being a virgin, prompting him to rape her several more times. Yorma didn't dare mention her father when her cousin found out she was pregnant and assumed it was by him. He began to take precautions and consider a possible solution, lest the news reach her father.

At one point, her father struck her in the stomach with a cane over and over until she passed out. But, with the fetus growing inside her belly, time was of the essence—and not to be wasted on fainting. He lit a rag on fire and brought it to her nose to wake her up, then let her rest for an hour. He resumed his assault on her stomach until she begrudgingly agreed to leave the house, with nowhere to go.

As Fares listened to her words, he cursed the scourge of ignorance and swore he'd work to bring the light of knowledge to these gloomy homes.

Yorma was unsure where to go, so she descended the sloping pathways and wandered desolate trails across the mountains and through the valleys. Hours later, she reached the Beirut-Damascus Road. She'd heard a lot about the road, the cities it connects, and the lodging and businesses along the way.

Drawn to the highway, Yorma set off toward Beirut. She was overwhelmed when she arrived, unsure which street to take or where to go. Night had fallen and Yorma, visibly pregnant, wept. She knocked on the door of a home from which she heard the cries of children. A woman with a kind mien answered and took pity on her. But Yorma remained silent, refusing to answer any of the woman's questions. The woman was concerned about getting mixed up in a situation she didn't need to be a part of, given what she heard from time to time about the crimes committed in Beirut, especially honor killings, and about women's bodies being dumped in places "behind the barracks" and in the surrounding areas. As such, she asked Yorma to leave the house immediately.

With tears streaming down her face, Yorma left the house feeling melancholic and lonesome. The night was cloudy and ominous, devoid of stars or moonlight. Before her was a muddy alleyway and intense darkness.

Fares imagined himself as a young boy at night with his mother and siblings, their father absent. He wondered how his mother would have reacted if a girl like Yorma had come knocking on their door. Would she have responded differently than the woman who turned Yorma away?

"This must not continue," Fares said to himself. "Ignorance is the root cause of this misery. Women make up half of society. A nation can't take flight with only one wing. Women are mothers, sisters, and wives to statesmen and luminaries. They are the bandages on our wounds. Women aren't bad luck: In sophisticated nations, they are as respected as men."

A month before, Fares was shaken to his core when their neighbor took her life after giving birth to a daughter instead of a son for the third time. Just before noon, he heard the sound of screaming coming from his neighbors' house, so he ran to investigate. Before she gave birth, the neighbor had prepared the poison in a glass she placed near her bed. When the midwife told her that her newborn was a girl, she took the glass and drained it in one gulp down to the dregs. Within minutes, she had slipped away into an eternal slumber—unable to bear her husband's cruelty or her relatives' scornful glares. Her husband had threatened to beat her if she gave birth to another girl. Fares wanted to save her with the medical knowledge he had acquired from various places, but he was not allowed to come in. It would have been improper for him to see her like this.

Yorma spent that night perturbed. Fatigue overcame her to the point that she found her way to a nunnery. She stood at the door, unable to find the courage to knock for fear they would turn her away! On the verge of collapsing from exhaustion, she wrapped herself up in her clothes and fell asleep.

When the door opened early in the morning, Yorma was awoken by a nun's voice calling her. She was barely conscious and felt pain in her head and belly.

"What's this blood?" the alarmed nun asked her.

Yorma was in so much pain that she hadn't been paying attention to anything. She followed the nun's gaze and saw that blood had soaked through her clothes below her abdomen. She felt something sticky between her thighs, then lost consciousness entirely. After some time, she awoke in bed in an empty room. An elderly nun who walked with a cane, her back hunched by age, was by her side.

"You had a miscarriage," she told Yorma, after reassuring her that she was recovering. "The fetus that was in your stomach is gone. You're fine now, thank the Lord. Tell me, who are you? Where are you from? Who's your husband?"

Yorma said nothing. Her silence was entirely reflexive, not intentional.

The nun told her that the nunnery would host her for the few days it would take for her to recover. After that, she had to leave.

"Why?" Fares demanded. "Why wouldn't you tell them what happened to you? They've taken vows of service to God's creatures."

"I was at a loss for words!" she replied. "I don't know. It wasn't something I was familiar with when I was thrown into that hell, at the age of thirteen."

After Yorma had recovered, the nuns gave her clothing and enough money to last a few days. They prayed for her safety, then sent her on her way.

Fares understood why the nuns acted as they did, but he couldn't grasp why Yorma stayed silent, why she didn't tell them what happened to her. They'd have surely helped her and found work for her, at the nunnery or elsewhere.

After leaving the nunnery, fate would have it that Yorma reached a hotel in Burj Square: the same square that, decades later, was renamed Martyrs' Square and became the heart of Beirut, the capital of the new Lebanese state.

The owner of the hotel, the Aman Inn, offered her work washing linens, dishes, and guests' clothes in exchange for food, housing, and a salary paid at the end of each week. Yorma wasted little time before agreeing, her heart filling with trepidation of this unknown fate and the new surroundings she found herself in. She hadn't done anything to deserve being mistreated like this.

When the owner of the motel asked about her name, her family, where she came from, whose daughter she was, and so on, she said nothing.

"Well, what am I supposed to call you?" he asked tersely.

"Yorma!" she replied.

She had no idea where this name had come from. She later found out that there was a food called "shawarma" and a shop called "Norma," and that the latter was a name for girls. She encountered many other names that she learned were foreign: from Europe or from America, that vast country across the ocean. Many people gave their children these names, as well as used foreign words when naming their shops as a sign of prestige and currency.

The owner of the motel brought her to a small, dirty, dimly lit room. "And this is where you'll stay!" he told her. Her eyes filled with tears. After he left, she kept crying in the dark until a conviction stirred within her, which she accepted without a second thought: She was not going to live there for long!

The room was dark even during the day, and only with great difficulty was Yorma able to find anything. On cloudy days, she had to light a candle. This went on for several weeks, until one day the owner came to her and said that an affluent man staying at the hotel was looking for a woman.

"Looking for a wife?" she prompted.

"No, of course not!" he said. "He's looking for a woman to spend time with before he goes to bed at night in return for a lot of money."

"And what would she be doing?"

The owner explained what she was to do in a roundabout way, but Yorma declined, having grown apprehensive—much to the owner's chagrin.

On the second and third occasions, however, he threatened to evict her unless she met the demands of his wealthy guests.

Only the wealthy ones.

This is how poor Yorma began her journey through the world of humiliation and sin, how she started earning a living in this degrading profession—how she was given a room with a window to let in fresh air and lots of sunlight. But the warm glow was tinged with the hues of remorse and guilt.

In those days, Yorma still pined for her village. She was able to keep up with the developments indirectly, lest her family find out about her. She knew her father and cousin were searching everywhere in a desperate attempt to cleanse the shame she had brought upon the family by getting pregnant by an unknown man, out of wedlock. She'd heard that someone matching her cousin's description was looking for her.

Then came the dispute between her and the hotel owner, who would incessantly demand more of her earnings from the rich clientele. Eventually, she left the hotel after secretly accepting a job with the owner of a salon patronized by sophisticated Beiruti men and those visiting the city. The owner taught Yorma how to look after a home, how to cook, and how to flatter the clients while they drank. Soon, however, the owner stopped her from interacting with special clients; to them, she assigned a tall, blonde European girl with a pretty face. The owner claimed that this girl was more comfortable in her body than Yorma, that she knew how to talk to clients and create the right atmosphere.

"You're still a village girl!" he reasoned.

Furious at this prejudice, Yorma left her work there and settled where Fares used to visit her "behind the barracks." She confided in him her overwhelming desire to rid herself of this demeaning occupation. She had lived in constant fear ever since she heard that some families from her village had moved to live and work in Beirut.

Before Fares had earned Yorma's trust and succeeded in convincing her to let him enter her, he used to rub his penis under her armpit until he reached orgasm. She didn't allow him to do anything else, and she used to charge more if her armpit area was "clean," meaning hairless from sugaring. The mouth, however, was off-limits: If a man's fluid entered the body from the wrong side, it would leave behind the seeds of tumors that would distort her body. It could even get a woman pregnant—no matter her age—with a malformed embryo.

"Can you imagine?" she asked him. "A woman my age, in her fifties or sixties, no husband, body misshapen, and pregnant with a disfigured child!"

But Fares convinced her that this belief was a superstition. He explained what that meant: an illusion of the unlearned imagination with no rational basis in reality. Even more, he assured her that a man's fluid is beneficial to the female body, especially the skin. He'd gotten this information from what he'd read and the things he'd heard from his older classmates. As a result, Yorma agreed to receive him in her mouth.

Fares told Jurji what happened, as well as his other close friends who began visiting her often to enjoy this practice themselves. This was a possible mistake on Fares's part, one that would torment him for a long time. A few months later, a rumor circulated that Yorma had been seen pregnant. When Fares heard about it, he went to see her and ask about it. But he couldn't find her.

She had disappeared!

All this happened as a locust outbreak ravaged the country. At the time, everyone, Fares included, was preoccupied with responding to the disaster.

# 9

One evening, in the fall of that same year, fiery meteors passing over Beirut caught people by surprise, nearly colliding with modern multistory buildings. Afterward, thunderstorms lasted the rest of the night, frightening people into their cellars. They hid their children in underground rooms, and some even dug below their houses as a hiding place. Churches, mosques, and synagogues were packed with fearful neighbors. When a meteor shower startled passersby, they would take shelter in the nearest place of worship. One would find fearful Christians, Muslim, and Jews under the same roof. Each of them believed that their neighbor's prayer would be their salvation. No longer was the prayer of one believer enough to stave off the cosmic downpour upon joyful Beirut; the prayer of other believers was now a vital form of support, as though filling a void.

The downpours caused the sewers to overflow, soiling streets and alleyways all across the burgeoning city with sewage. This flood lasted only a few hours, after which the skies cleared and the temperature rose, drying the land. The filth began to emit foul odors as it dried, and harmful microbes spread. Typhoid broke out, claiming the lives of dozens of children and the elderly.

Had these conditions made it easier for opportunists to make Yorma disappear, for fear that she'd give birth to a monstrosity after having consumed the male emission? Weren't the locusts, the meteor showers, the floods, the plagues all due to God's anger at man's depravity?

Fares knew that the College of Medicine was in constant need of cadavers so the students could learn anatomy, and he knew that no one in Beirut, in nearby Mount Lebanon, nor anywhere in Greater Syria would consent to give his body or that of a relative to the university to be desecrated. One must respect the dead. He knew that the emperor of Brazil had been given an evasive response.

Fares also knew that, without gross anatomy, no student would be able to graduate with a diploma to practice medicine anywhere in the empire. The exam that permitted doctors to practice was held in Istanbul, not in Beirut, so neither the university administration nor the students could avoid this difficulty. Anatomy must be taught.

Fares also knew that cadavers had to be brought to the university from somewhere nearby, so as not to deteriorate before arrival.

The mystery was, thus, close at hand—and thinly veiled.

Fares felt guilty. He worried that his prattle had allowed the unscrupulous to learn that she had accepted a man in her mouth.

The greater paradox was that this practice became immensely popular at the time—far more so than after the French military reached the shores of Beirut in 1860, when many brothels sprang up to meet the needs of thousands of French sailors.

This time, the practice gradually began to reach married couples. Wives would tell their neighbors about its pleasant effect, and men would discuss it with their friends.

Some historians of the practice report that, within a few years, it had spread among the towns and villages of Syria and the whole of the Ottoman Empire. Couples enjoyed it and became much more sexually active. Women liked it because it gave them an advantage over their husbands and made it easier for them to switch roles.

Historians also note that it became less common for husbands to stay out at night, and infidelity rates declined.

Beirut's temperament in the 1870s changed as this practice proliferated—less than ten years after the College of Medicine was founded at the American University, and on the eve of the opening of a medical school at the Jesuit Saint Joseph University. Historians agree that in this period the city saw an outgrowth of activity never before seen in its history. Of course, they attribute this significant transformation to a variety of reasons, not to this factor alone.

And though Fares was proud to have contributed actively to this development, Yorma's disappearance marred his joy.

# 10

After vanishing for five whole years, Fares's father resurfaced. He wrote to them announcing that he was alive, that he had reached New York and settled there, that work was going better than expected, that he was in good health, and that he was living in his own room in a multiroom apartment on Washington Street—over there, the streets had names, like people. Each one had its own. In America they named streets after their rulers, their military leaders, and their towering figures in philosophy, literature, the arts, and all other fields.

In his letters, he'd kept repeating that he'd be back in two or three years, after having saved up enough money to buy a house in Beirut and start a business: a shop that made Western shoes. Everyone in America wore shoes. You wouldn't see a single person there barefoot, whether rich or poor, man or woman, young or old. Shoes there came in all sorts of colors. Most were black, but red and brown were also common—even strange colors, like yellow and blue. Over there, you'd find ankle-high boots as well as mid-rise shoes, which were the most fashionable of all. Shoemaking had a future anywhere in Greater Syria and the East.

After making contact, Mansour resumed sending money to the family, renewing Fares's faith in his future. He was glad that his father had returned, although his happiness was tarnished by the dismay of having developed a taste for total freedom from all forms of fatherly supervision. He was particularly pleased that he would at last achieve his dream of becoming a doctor, of taking part in spreading happiness throughout Beirut: this steadily blossoming city, the pearl of the Mediterranean's eastern coast . . . despite the setback it had suffered, which had led to dear Yorma's disappearance.

People's bodies would become a source of joy, not cause for fear and anxiety.

Fares's children would go to the same school as his friend Saadeddine's children. Religious differences wouldn't drive them away from one another: Their diversity would bring them together and enrich them.

The same homeland would unite them!

Mansour was still eager to realize his dream through his son. This was the first thing he wrote in his letter, after offering his greetings and expressing his homesickness and the reason for his absence.

It was in this way that Fares's affairs came together, setting him on the route that he believed would undoubtedly take him to medicine.

His friend Jurji, on the other hand, had made the fateful decision to specialize in medicine no matter the difficulties and managed to complete the two-year preparatory stage in only two months! Over the summer, his professor Iskandar Baroudi gave him private lessons in natural philosophy, algebra, geometry, arithmetic, Arabic grammar, and English: subjects that were taught over the course of two years before taking the medical school entrance exams, which Jurji passed.

And so it was that Fares and Jurji were reunited in the lecture halls of the American University.

One day during their first year, Fares and Jurji met their friend Jamil al-Helou, a third-year medical student. He told them the college was in dire need of cadavers.

Fares, who was unwavering in his conviction that medicine had a central role to play in the country's advancement, was perturbed. But at that moment, he needed to overcome his shock and apprehension so that the college could keep going and its students could pass the licensing exams held in Istanbul. It was a national issue.

He recalled Yorma.

His aunt, Imm Shahed, was one of the few whose circumstances had led them to die in the hospital. One of her relatives was taking care of her: an unmarried woman who looked after the members of her family whose children had migrated—who, as it were, became her inadvertent children themselves.

Imm Shahed had been ill for months, during which she remained at home. Days before she passed away, she was moved to the hospital, contrary to the customs of the time. This was after Fares got involved and persuaded her and her family that, in her present condition, the most suitable place for her to be was in the hospital.

It was a jarring surprise for Imm Shahed when she noticed the irony: In her illness, she was being taken *away* from her house to another place (a hospital, of all places!) even though the ailing are supposed to rest at home. What better a place for a person to die, after all, than at home, in their own bed?

While all of this was happening, Jamil complained that the university was no longer receiving cadavers, causing major problems that were sure to have repercussions for the future of the college, the students, and the entire country.

Fares and Jamil deliberated the matter together, then spoke to Jurji. The three devised a trick to reroute the body of Fares's aunt after her death from the church to the university instead of the graveyard. This was no easy decision for Fares—but desperate times called for desperate measures.

The family burial ground was still in the public graveyard in the village, in the mountains: a day's journey by mule from Beirut.

The plot began to unfold just before Imm Shahed's death. Fares sent for Hanna, caretaker of the village graveyard, and asked him to dig a grave for Imm Shahed, the wife of his uncle Semaan; to purchase her a coffin and leave it near the grave; then to set out at once for Beirut by mule, no matter the cost, to bring the body for burial alongside her parents and relatives. And so, the next day, Hanna arrived by mule.

The second step required Fares, Jamil, and Jurji to forge legal paperwork that would allow them to give the body to the university. This was very easy, since Fares was closer to the deceased than anyone in Lebanon and was therefore authorized to carry out all related legal procedures. He forged a document stating that, upon her death, she would donate her body to the College of Medicine at the American University for the public good.

The next step was to trick Hanna and prepare two identical loads: one containing the body, and the other containing sawdust mixed with soil and some branches that resembled the limbs and head, wrapped in cloth.

Imm Shahed had already died by the time Hanna arrived. They told him the funeral had been held at the hospital chapel.

"Hospital?" he repeated, perplexed.

They explained to Hanna what a hospital was. He was amazed. But sadness swiftly overshadowed his amazement when he considered the prospect of someone dying far from home, among strangers, in a hospital. He cursed migration for leaving this woman without a spouse or children, robbing her of her deathbed at home.

Hanna was a simple man of borderline intelligence, and getting things by him was quite easy.

They then set out as a group—Hanna, Fares, Jurji, and the mule carrying the body—to bury Imm Shahed. Jamil had already arrived at the Damour River, where he waited with a mule that was carrying the decoy load.

It was there at the resting place along the Damour that Fares and Jurji outwitted Hanna. They tied up the mule with the body in a secluded area behind the resthouse, then fed Hanna grilled meat the likes of which he'd never tasted before in his life (at the time, such a portion of meat was beyond the means of the common people). They gave him a glass of *arak* to drink, then another, and he sat down to relax as he ate, gazing at the flowing water and daydreaming about who knows what.

While Fares stayed with Hanna, Jurji went over to Jamil next to the mule carrying the decoy beside the other mule, which carried the body. The two quickly swapped the loads, so the body was placed on Jamil's mule and the decoy on Hanna's. Then Jurji came and told Fares, in front of Hanna, that he was heading back to Beirut with some other travelers, bade them goodbye, and left.

Thus Jurji and Jamil set out for Beirut with the body, and Fares and Hanna proceeded to the village with the decoy. They reached the graveyard at sunset, having circumnavigated the village to get there. Fares had insisted there was no use in bothering people at such a time, when they were returning home from their fields and workplaces.

As soon as they reached the grave, next to which lay the coffin, Fares asked Hanna to hold the reins to keep the mule from moving. Right away, he unfastened the decoy from the mule's back with such reckless haste that he nearly tripped and fell into the hole. He managed to regain his balance and placed the "body" in the coffin before Hanna could come around to help him. He closed it and, with Hanna's help, lowered it down into the grave.

"Come on, get shoveling!" said Fares.

"Without a priest?"

What sense did it make to bury someone without having a priest pray for them?

Hanna was unfamiliar with this new burial method. It was contrary to his usual practices. Until that point, he had deferred to Fares, the educated young man from the city who knew how people in advanced countries behave. But the final prayer was a necessity only a priest could fulfill.

"Bury her without a priest?! We've got to send for a priest!" Hanna insisted. Everything has its limits.

The custom in the village was for a priest to pray for the deceased as their body was placed in the grave, before being covered with dirt and hidden away below the earth for eternity.

As Fares began shoveling the dirt, Hanna watched for a time. Then without warning he began to wail like a hyena, as the villagers sometimes called him, and ran off toward the village. Fares ran after him as fast as he could, worried that the hyena would call for the priest and the villagers and his trick would be revealed. Things would soon get out of hand. But Fares was too late: The villagers had already begun to gather around Hanna, who told them that Imm Shahed had been buried before a priest could pray over her.

Night had fallen, and it was widely accepted that the dead stalk the living at night and could harm them, if they wished. But this didn't stop some of the villagers, including several relatives of the deceased, from going with the priest to the graveyard.

On the way there, Fares explained to them that the funeral had already taken place and that he could have buried her in the city, but he preferred to bury her here in her village, close to her late parents and her living relatives, who would keep her company. They all respected his devotion to his village and were impressed by his forthrightness.

Fares reached the grave before them and, to divert suspicion, called for Hanna to bring him the shovel and remove the soil on top of the coffin, so he could open it. His ploy was a success: No one called his bluff, as people rarely wanted to see dead bodies—much less at night. The priest assured him that there was no need, and that he could perform the prayer as things were right before they filled her grave with soil.

In this way, Fares escaped his predicament, and the decoy was buried in place of his aunt. He returned with the priest and the group to the village and accepted condolences at a relative's house, where he slept.

# 11

Fares awoke at dawn and set out for Beirut, with a burning curiosity to learn what had happened there.

The body, as it turned out, still hadn't reached the college's dissection hall! Numerous reports had circulated that bodies were disappearing in Beirut, and that it had to do with the medical students' need for cadavers. It was a great embarrassment for the Ottoman authorities at the time. So, to reassure people, they set up a checkpoint at the university's eastern gate from time to time. Unfortunately for Fares and his companions, on that very day the checkpoint was in place, which made it impossible for Jurji and Jamil to deliver the body. The administration, faculty, and students gathered that these checkpoints were a kind of warning and cause for greater attentiveness and caution. They were all aware of the rampant corruption among the city's Ottoman personnel. They knew that everything, no matter how illegal, had a price—but also that everything had its limits.

The sun had begun to set when an exhausted Fares arrived home in Beirut, where his friends were waiting for him. They had no idea what to do with the body, still on the back of the mule tied up behind the house, and they informed a perplexed Imm Fares that they'd hired the mule to move some of the college's furniture.

In the meantime, Jurji went to see Saadeddine to discuss the matter and asked his advice. But Saadeddine's rank wasn't enough for him to give the order to remove the checkpoint.

Jurji and Jamil were especially worried about the foul odor that the body would begin to emit if things went on too long like this. It was April: The days were long and the sun was intense. People went out; they didn't stay inside all day. All of this was cause for concern.

Yusuf Yacoub, professor of anatomy at the time, was a regular at Abu Jurji's restaurant. He would order a plate of beans with an onion, light on garlic, heavy on the oil, and lots of bread.

(In those days, it was not widely known that eating a lot of bread causes obesity. America did not have the kind of presence in the world or in Beirut that it has today, nor did millions of those living there suffer from obesity.)

Jurji himself used to prepare the meal for his professor, who had taken notice of his intelligence and capability. He was fond of Fares, too, and often invited them to join him. The three would talk about medicine, the college, and the difficulties it was facing in teaching anatomy, due to the shortage of cadavers.

The professor, it seemed, was their solution. They set out for Yacoub's house without giving Fares—so tired that he was staggering—the chance to rest even for an hour.

Though Professor Yacoub was unsettled when they presented the situation to him, in truth he could hardly contain his glee, because of the difficulties they were facing at the university with the shortage of cadavers. At the same time, he was anxious that the secret would come to light and he would find himself in an awkward position with the Ottoman authorities in the city and the administration, which always requested that faculty exercise the utmost caution in this matter. He was worried that people would learn of his involvement, given how concerned they were about their dead. Within a few years, this fear would reach such an extent that many people hired guards to watch over their relatives' graves for a long enough period so that they could be sure the body had begun to decompose and was no longer worth stealing for dissection. The recently established press in Beirut mentioned the issue periodically, in papers such as *Lisán al-Hal* and *Thamarát al-Funún*.

After a moment of apprehension, the professor got up and changed into his work clothes, then asked them to wait for him to return shortly with a horse-drawn cart after ensuring that the checkpoint had been removed.

Thus the body finally reached its destination, severely discolored, but in one piece. Neither the students nor the faculty asked where the cadavers came from; they were happy with what they received and would begin work without question.

Although Fares didn't take part in those anatomy lessons, he had a sense of his importance after this incident. It was the second time that he felt he had value and a role to play, that he could affect the course of events and take part in making the history of his city and country.

The first time he felt this way was when he helped lift the veils of ignorance from the human body and spread a kind of joy that would come to define the mood of the city—even though the cost was Yorma's disappearance.

Fares was aware of the case of Dr. Edwin Lewis. In early 1882, Lewis served wine to his guests, contrary to the habits of the missionaries, who didn't consume any alcohol and who criticized him harshly for doing so. But he didn't grasp the depth of the conflict that this affair entailed.

And although Fares had learned about Darwin's theory before going to university, he was unaware of its gravity. At university, however, the theory had its proponents, most notably the young professor William van Dyck, son of the famed Cornelius van Dyck who healed his father within hours. He was a priest, a scientist, and a teacher who taught medicine in Arabic, which he spoke as well as a native. He was generous and considerate, and he believed in equality between races, cultures, and religions. His students loved him and sang his praises. His fame spread all across Syria, of whose people he was truly fond, to such an extent that it was widely believed that he had founded the university and its medical school: Many people used to call it the "Van Dyck College"!

William van Dyck, son of Cornelius, who spoke Arabic like a Beiruti, had studied to be a doctor in America. He was appointed an instructor at the medical school in 1880: the year Fares came to the university.

The young physician, scientist, and professor was devoted to his research and especially enamored of Charles Darwin's new theory about the origin and development of species. He obtained all of Darwin's books and articles, read them thoughtfully, then gave them to his students to read and discuss. This theory was not only the talk of students in the College of Medicine but in all the university's fields. Soon, the discussion spread throughout educated and intellectual circles in Beirut and all of Syria—even reaching academics and journalists in Cairo, too.

Reverberations of this discussion reached the masses, who took a great liking to it. The theory as they understood it became the source of dozens of jokes. Sometimes, these jokes became ways for sects to express how they felt about one another. The Sunni's grandfather was a camel (because Islam comes from the desert), the Maronite's grandfather a goat (because the Maronites live in the mountains), the Shi'i's grandfather a cow (because cows are melancholy animals), the Druze's a bull (because of its steadfastness), the Orthodox's a horse (because of its cleanliness), the Protestant's a tomcat (because they had similar eyes), and so on.

Because he followed the latest research at European and American universities, Dr. van Dyck made his students feel they were affecting change at the heart of the action. They grew passionate about their country, their city, their university. Aware of his father's love of knowledge and of the nation, Fares wrote to Mansour, telling him to gather his money and his things and come back to Beirut to bear witness to its transformation into a scientific hub and a cultural beacon on par with Cairo—and soon to overtake Paris!

Fares was so caught up with these things that he would forget to mention in his letters the declining health of his mother, who had begun to experience trouble breathing, chest pain, and headaches. Fares wrote regularly to keep his father apprised of scholarly developments. In one such letter from early 1882, he wrote that their professor, Dr. Willam van Dyck, was in contact with the English scientist Charles Darwin himself. Fares was telling the truth: One day, van Dyck, captivated by Darwin, wished to investigate (and validate) his theory, so he began a comprehensive study titled "On the Modification of a Race of Syrian Street Dogs by Means of Sexual Selection." He formulated the study into an article and sent it to Darwin, asking him to publish it in a magazine or newspaper, should he see fit. But Darwin was ill the day he received the letter and was unable to respond, so he asked one of his children to reply and thank the sender on his behalf.

Darwin, after recovering, was pleased when he read the study. He wrote back to van Dyck to that effect, informing him that upon consideration he had decided to send the article to the Zoological Society and ask them to publish it. Darwin also told him that he had "seen fit" to make a few comments on the article and that, if the society declined to publish it, he found it promising enough to send to *Nature*, the most important scientific magazine of the day.

Dr. van Dyck told his students about this correspondence and, naturally, let them see the letters. All of them, Fares most of all, were in disbelief as to what they were hearing and seeing. They eagerly awaited the day their professor would announce that his article had been published, and they didn't hesitate to ask him if there was news each time they saw him.

But their professor would always remind them that publishing an article in a journal or a newspaper took a long time—months, if not more.

The same day the professor told his dumbfounded students about the letter Darwin himself had written to him, Fares asked his permission to make a copy of it right away. Van Dyck agreed, and Fares made several copies. He sent one to his father, to show him "how far along our country was getting on the road to progress and advancement!" His father responded with more encouragement to learn and persevere, to serve his country, and to contribute as much as possible to the great national revival, in which all must take part—old and young, women and men . . . everyone in their own way: the peasant in the field, the worker in the factory, the teacher in the schoolhouse.

The American Protestant missionaries, especially the first ones to reach the Syrian coasts, firmly believed that the world "will last 1,000 years but not 2,000 years"—that the end of days would come with the approach of the year 2000—and that there was a pressing need to convert the Christians and Muslims of the East to Protestantism. But Beirut's intellectual vanguard, along with their counterparts in other Syrian cities and in Cairo, firmly believed that it was *backwardness* that would "last 1,000 years but not 2,000 years." They were certain that a brighter future was nigh, that the sun would soon illuminate the shadows; that a new dawn would emerge from the darkness of sheer ignorance and odious fanaticism; that knowledge would prevail against myth and superstition; that religion belongs to God and the homeland belongs to all; that the different religions and sects would unite in peace under the banner of the new, all-encompassing homeland; and that the nation would continue to advance until soon gaining equal footing with its European neighbors.

The unfortunate thing about the article's publication is that on April 19, 1882, a mere sixteen days after writing to William van Dyck on April 3, Darwin passed away. It was a somber day for van Dyck and his students when the news arrived. They had lost an inspiration, an asset to all of mankind. It was even as if they had lost an ally, one of their own—a fellow countryman, a Syrian, an Easterner.

The students vowed to maintain a connection with Darwin, despite his passing, by reading his books and articles, discussing them, delving into them, working and studying in their spirit. At their aid was their professor, who shared an unbreaking spiritual attachment to the late scholar.

With some effort, Fares managed to obtain a portrait of Darwin. He hung it up, beside Darwin's final letter to the professor, on the wall above his bed.

# 12

Just three months after Darwin's death, another earthquake shook the students' resolve and weakened their confidence in the missionaries. What followed was the first student strike in the East—perhaps in all of Asia and Africa. On Wednesday, July 19, at ten o'clock in the morning, a graduation ceremony was held for a class of the college's medical, pharmacy, and science students. Dr. Edwin Lewis was commissioned by the administration to give the main speech. It was this very address that ignited the upheaval that would later be known as the Darwin affair.

Lewis made several points during his farewell to the students, in particular urging them to distinguish between knowledge and science. Mere knowledge is inferior to science, not equivalent to it. While knowledge happens simply by paying attention to phenomena, science uncovers their underlying causes and interrelations.

Dr. Lewis gave two examples of this point. The first, which had no ramifications and elicited no reaction, was the book *Principles of Geology*, published in 1833 by the English geologist Sir Charles Lyell. The second, which triggered the crisis, was *On the Origin of Species* by the naturalist Charles Darwin, published in 1859, which explored the causes that produced, over the course of generations, the great divergence among the flora and fauna we see today. In the address, Lewis criticized those who argue that this school of thought is contrary to religion, because God is the original cause of all things. He invited the students not to shy away from the facts and reassured them that those who seek to uncover the secrets of nature in search of truth are doing nothing wrong.

Fares wasn't surprised by this part of the speech because he already knew it. He'd heard of this theory before entering university, then spent two full years delving into it at a time when students of all kinds were discussing it widely.

What he was hearing from Dr. Lewis was significantly less radical than what he used to hear from Dr. van Dyck.

What did surprise him, though, was the reaction of the administration and the conservative faculty, who caused quite a commotion. He and his friends became aware that the president of the university, Dr. Daniel Bliss, had confided in some professors that Dr. Lewis's speech contradicted what the scripture has to say about the creation of the world and had endorsed Darwin's theory without scientifically investigating its veracity first.

In this way, the wine on Dr. Lewis's table and, a few months later, his promotion of Darwin's theory on the origin of species at a public event ignited a pent-up conflict between the conservative and liberal camps of the foreign missionaries and faculty.

So the crisis began. It continued to build until Dr. Lewis was forced to tender his resignation and deliver it to the board of trustees in New York, which met and resolved to accept it on December 1, 1882. A telegram reached Beirut the next day conveying that the resignation had been accepted, effective immediately.

Dr. Lewis's resignation had a profoundly jarring effect on the students, who immediately declared an open-ended strike to have him reinstated. They took the opportunity to make other demands related to their future, including the exam language. At the end of their final year, students were required to take an exam before a special committee in Istanbul. It had previously been held in Arabic, but then the Ottoman authorities decided to hold it in either Turkish or French.

At the time, students at the college studied in Arabic, and they were not necessarily proficient in Turkish or French. Thus, they faced a serious dilemma that put their careers in jeopardy. The college used to hold an assessment to grant students authorization to apply for the exam in Istanbul. Yet the students called for this first exam to be canceled, as they would have to take the second anyway.

The exam in Istanbul also contained material not covered by the college curriculum. Naturally, the students wanted to be taught this information and close this gap.

These demands, despite their importance, were not what caused the crisis. The administration was rather sympathetic to such concerns and worked with the students to address them. Instead, the issue that led to the strike (which would never have been declared without it) was Dr. Lewis's removal from his post at the college. The students objected to the administration's position on two grounds: that Lewis's dismissal in the middle of the semester meant losing a competent chemistry instructor who could not easily be replaced, and that their esteemed professor had been fired in a manner unbefitting for the elevated regard in which they held him.

Lewis's liberalism and, in their view, service to the homeland constituted the main motivation for their mobilization. One of their petitions included a critique of the administration for not having taken into account the professor's contributions to "our country"!

Liberalism, patriotism, and progressivism were, for this generation of Syrian and Arab intellectuals, inseparable characteristics.

Alongside the liberals, students of all sects took a clear stance against the college administration, from which they were met with immense intransigence. As the struggle escalated, there was much give and take: messages received and rebuttals launched, ultimatums imposed and summarily disregarded.

Fares wholeheartedly supported the student movement, which was a national renaissance to him as much as it was to the rest of the students. But his mother's declining health prevented him from joining and assuming responsibilities in the vanguard of resistance to fulfill the students' just demands.

As Imm Fares began to fall ill, Fares had been preoccupied with Darwin's theory and Dr. van Dyck's correspondence with the English naturalist. He thought of the letters as a direct link between Darwin and himself. The news of Darwin's death on April 19 caused him to forget about his mother entirely. He wept alongside his companions at the university, all of whom were Darwinists, as well as his friend Saadeddine of the Ottoman police force.

Darwin had unwittingly become an ally of Beirut's educated nationalist vanguard—in life and death alike. When he died, the students held a memorial at Abu Jurji's restaurant. Darwin's passing was to be an occasion for numerous gatherings at which his contributions were discussed.

There was much emphasis on the role Darwin's theory would play in deepening humanity's awareness of its essence and history. In attendance were Drs. van Dyck and Lewis, the latter of whom asked, for purely practical reasons, that his presence be kept a secret, so as not to further strain his relations with the administration, given his support for Darwin's theory and the wine he served.

Saadeddine, who had recently been promoted to the rank of officer, attended many of these meetings and provided security.

Because Darwin's theory had been the reason for Dr. Lewis's resignation—which was the main cause of the strike, not the other issues on which the administration agreed—the students delved deeper into it. At each meeting, they presented what they had read and the information they gathered from the European and American journals they had access to. The more they discussed and immersed themselves in this theory, the more they became convinced of it, and the greater their confidence grew in the strike they had declared.

At one of the meetings, Fares and his companions speculated as to whether Darwin would have consented to offer his body for dissection at one of London's medical colleges, had he been asked. A lengthy discussion of the issue ensued, through which they arrived at no clear conclusions. Dr. van Dyck was of the opinion that whatever Darwin's answer, it had no effect, positive or negative, on the importance of his theory to the understanding of the evolution and diversity of plant and animal species.

Afterward, when Fares returned home to check on his mother, he was taken aback by how much worse her condition had become.

He felt as if he had been struck, as within a mere two years he would become a doctor after graduating from an American university, the second oldest in the whole Arab world after Qasr El Eyni in Cairo.

Claiming to be preparing medicine, Fares secluded himself in a corner of the house and cried alone in the darkness.

Her heart was about to give out, and her lungs had filled with fluid, due to heart failure. He knew she would soon go into a coma, in a matter of hours or days at the most.

He cried out of guilt and regret. Wasn't he studying medicine to heal the people of his country and ease their suffering? How, then, could he have neglected his duties toward his own mother?

But what alleviated his sense of guilt and regret was that his siblings, who would come visit him from time to time, kept him informed about his mother's condition to stave off his anxiety and keep him from falling behind in his studies. They were excited that he would be graduating as a physician in a city, if not a country, with scarcely any doctors. They seemed to think that the fact alone that their brother was specializing in medicine was enough to protect them and their mother from sickness and death.

Fares may have cried, but he didn't give in to his tears. He immediately set off to work, in the manner of those Westerners who taught him, who didn't break down in front of disasters. He went to the college and asked the medical faculty for help, as his knowledge and experience weren't enough to handle this case. Dr. van Dyck offered to help right away. On the way, as they rode in the carriage, Fares explained the situation to his professor and gave his judgment.

Upon examination, his professor reached the same conclusion. Fares was pleased and felt a boost of self-confidence. But, soon enough, his sorrows returned when he remembered that it was in relation to his own mother.

It was late at night as the two stood outside the door discussing the matter, and Fares was deeply distressed. Mere hours before, he had been with Dr. van Dyck at the meeting to discuss Darwin and his theory. He himself participated in the conversation about what Darwin would have done had he been asked to donate his body to be dissected for the sake of science, knowledge, the university, and its students—for the nation. There was a shortage of bodies at the university, and the final examination—or "Judgment Day," as the students called it—was to take place in the capital Istanbul.

Fares was of the opinion that if he were in Darwin's place and had been asked to make such a sacrifice, he would have undoubtedly agreed. He made this known in front of everyone and justified his views at length, in a bid to convince those who had yet to make up their minds.

Fares's unease was immense as he spoke with his professor in front of the door. Were his love of country and his sense of service toward the university so great that he would donate his own mother's body for dissection? How was he supposed to visit her grave, to lay down a bouquet of flowers—how was he supposed to mourn her if her body were destroyed? Aren't the graveyards scattered on the fringes of villages the roots from which communities draw life? Aren't the dead the foundation of our towns and cities? Isn't trifling with death tantamount to trifling with life itself?

Wasn't it enough that he'd given his aunt's body for dissection?

It was an uncomfortable moment for both of them. Dr. van Dyck had also been at the meeting and surely recalled what had happened there, particularly what Fares had said, but neither of them expressed their thoughts aloud. An intense, silent dialogue raged between them and within each of them. Fares felt earnestly trapped: Should he come out and say what was on his mind?

He resolved to give himself some time, lest he make a hasty decision and regret it. He didn't want to act on something of such gravity before asking the opinion of his friend Jurji, who, having come to play an active and essential part in the strike, was extremely preoccupied at the time. During the students' first general assembly at the Prussian Hospital, where they used to train, Jurji was selected to head the ten-member committee tasked with organizing the strike.[1]

Fares spent the following day with his mother. In the evening, he visited the university to inform Jurji of what was going on and seek his advice, but no one in the dormitory wing could tell him Jurji's whereabouts. Eventually, he found his way to the shop run by Saadeddine's father, where the strikers were meeting in secret to discuss developments. Saadeddine used to invite them to his father's shop to protect them from prying eyes and from the dirty looks of the more conservative Christian and Muslim clerics, who were uncomfortable with what they'd begun to hear about the students' connection to Darwinism. By virtue of his position, Saadeddine stayed up-to-date on the course of events.

1. Today the American University of Beirut Medical Center (AUBMC).

Saadeddine didn't feel that Darwin's theory directly mattered to him from an academic perspective, but the idea amazed him nonetheless. It had invigorated his imagination, and he appreciated its novelty, as someone who wished for fresh air to flow through every mind and into every alleyway in Beirut. He was proud of his city and dreamt of it becoming the pearl of the Mediterranean. He did what he could to make the strikes a success.

By nature of his profession and his insight into happenings in the city, Saadeddine was a major pillar of support for the demonstrators. For instance, he once implored the strikers not to accept their colleague's proposal to form local committees with a mix of all sects to support the strike, pressure the administration, and instill a scientific awareness in the public all at once. Saadeddine convinced them that this would raise the suspicion of the higher Ottoman authorities in Beirut and drive them to take a stand against the strike. The level of awareness of the common people didn't yet allow the formation of this kind of a support network. He also cautioned them against underestimating the university administration's American homeland.

All the students knew who this country was, and that it had stationed warships on the eastern shores of the Mediterranean. Everyone was aware of the time the captain of one of these ships warned Ottoman officials in Homs against preventing an American missionary from opening a school in a village near the shore. The prohibition had come at the request of Christian and Muslim religious leaders. In a telegram, the American captain threatened to strike the city if the authorities didn't recant the decision. And so they did. The press didn't cover the event at the time, as newspapers used to avoid printing or commenting on such stories to avert any potential problems with the Ottoman authorities. Despite this, the news spread throughout Beirut's American community and reached all areas of the Sultanate where Americans were living for whatever reason.

Officially, the United States of America would support the administration if need be. It certainly wasn't going to help a bunch of liberal teachers who loved the country they lived in and their students. Nor would it come to the aid of students defying an administration made up of Westerners who had left their homeland—America, of all places!—to live somewhere thousands of miles away and civilize a miserable populace, who were no match for the rampant ignorance, sickness, and delusion that beset them. The strikers were well aware of this, so Saadeddine had little difficulty convincing them. They decided not to gamble with making the issue known far and wide, lest they give the high authorities in Istanbul—or the Americans—a reason to intervene, especially after one of the rebellious students suggested assassinating Dr. Bliss, president of the university, and announced that he was willing to carry out the task himself.

It was a clamorous meeting. Fares was torn between a desire to fully participate and concern for his ailing mother. He wanted to take part in this historic moment, this turning point in the annals of Greater Syria, this monumental leap toward the country's promising future. At the same time, he needed to be with his mother, who had dedicated her life to him and his siblings, who spared no means nor effort for him to continue his studies. Hadn't she sacrificed all they had? Hadn't she spent all those years cleaning houses? Hadn't she quietly encouraged him to leave his work as a stonemason with his uncles?

Because Jurji was chairing the meeting, Fares was unable to talk to him and had to wait until afterward. Fares was troubled on the way back to their adjacent homes, and he told Jurji that the end was near for his mother.

Jurji said nothing, which was unsurprising to Fares. It isn't easy to find the right words in such a situation, especially when one already knows what is going to happen. Mere days before the Darwin affair, the college was in need of a complete human skeleton. Students used to buy any assorted bone fragments they could find, but they hadn't managed to obtain a full skeleton. They would either purchase these bones at exorbitant prices or pilfer what they could from graveyards, especially at night.

At that point, Fares and Jurji would bide their time, with the help of Saadeddine al-Jabawi, then go to churches and mosques all over Beirut to find out about recent deaths. One day, Saadeddine came to them with good news: One of his young relatives, a sixteen-year-old girl, had passed away and was buried in Raml, south of the city. Thrilled at the prospect, Fares and Jurji went with him to the graveyard at sunset to find the grave's exact location. Then they sought out their friend Amin Fleihan, a third-year student who was very passionate about the university and its significance for the country's advancement, and devised a plan.

Late at night, the three of them—Saadeddine didn't wish to take part in exhuming his relative's body—went to the graveyard in a hired carriage. They proceeded toward the grave, which they had identified at sunset, and dug it up, using pickaxes and shovels. But all they found was old bones.

They had made a mistake.

They were terrified: not only of the dead, but also of someone discovering them.

Grave-digging at night, their whispers muffled by the sound of waves crashing at sea, was a horrifying proposition. They may not have believed in ghosts, but, in moments like these, even imaginary ghosts were petrifying. After finding the right grave, removing the girl's body, and placing it in a bag, they began filling the grave back up when, all of a sudden, a ghost materialized before their eyes!

Of course, it wasn't actually a ghost: It was the graveyard's groundskeeper, carrying not a rifle, but a cane. He took a few steps forward to see what was happening, then Jurji shrieked. The groundskeeper stopped in his tracks, dropped the cane, and took off running. Fares and Amin froze in place, dumbstruck.

Eventually, they managed to escape their predicament with the cargo. Though it had been a terrifying ordeal, their determination was unflagging, and they kept on the lookout for opportunities to obtain more cadavers.

"Saadeddine was happy to provide the body of a young member of his family—and he's a police officer," Fares thought to himself. "So why should we—the students, the ones directly involved—refuse to donate the bodies of our family members?"

But it was his own mother this time.

How was he supposed to learn anatomy using his mother's body?! It would be inhumane. Jurji suggested, in the event that he decided to donate his mother's body, that he make arrangements with the faculty and administration to postpone taking the anatomy course for several months.

Fares felt that Jurji was being insensitive, but he didn't tell him so. He knew Jurji had thought it over dispassionately and logically: He wasn't being coldhearted, but simply speaking out of concern for their future, the future of the college, and the of country. This capacity for objective, rational thought was one of the skills the students used to acquire from their foreign instructors. They considered it a sophisticated virtue that was beneficial when cultivating a modern temperament—for the good of the nation.

But she was his mother.

The ongoing strike gave Fares additional time to clear his mind and think calmly. Eventually, his devotion to his principles and the belief that one must give up what matters most for the good of the nation overcame his inherited sense of respect for the dead. His long rumination on the matter led him to conclude that this reverence shouldn't run counter to the national interest. Honoring the dead is a noble duty, but respecting the homeland's interests is nobler.

If a man were willing to sacrifice himself at the altar of the homeland, how could he withhold his mother's body?

Hadn't Jurji made a similar sacrifice? Hadn't the child's body that arrived last year belonged to one of Jurji's cousins? Hadn't he overlooked the time one Saturday when he came back home from the university and his mother told him that the body of his nine-year-old cousin had been stolen just hours after the burial? Hadn't he personally led his comrades to the grave? Isn't the road to national progress paved with sacrifices like that?

The logical thing for Fares to do, then, was to donate his mother's body to the college. Time was moving swiftly, the future of his generation was at stake, and the nation was calling. But Fares, who had made this deduction by himself, didn't reveal it to anyone, giving himself the opportunity to let time take its course.

# 13

At last, Fares was liberated from his plight. Amid the ongoing strikes and an intractable crisis, Imm Fares passed away on December 16, 1882. That particular day was a crucial moment in the course of the strikes, because the board of trustees had convened for a meeting. Most of them were Americans scattered across Greater Syria for missionary work or other purposes, and they had come to Beirut for this very reason.

Three days prior to the meeting, on December 13, the students gathered and drafted a detailed list of grievances. They signed their names and decided to present it to the board of trustees on the day of their meeting. Fares was present and had signed the petition.

A few hours before meeting with the board, however, the students held a second meeting. They composed another statement on the back of the first one, which included an unequivocal condemnation of both the president of the university, Dr. Bliss, and Dr. Post.

The reason for the emergency meeting was that the students had found out about the efforts that Dr. Bliss and Dr. Post were making to turn the trustees against the students—to present the latter as agitators that needed to be shown some manners.

Fares wasn't around for this impromptu gathering, on account of his mother's death the very same day, meaning that he didn't sign the second, more scathing statement.

The outcome of the meeting with the board of trustees was that students who had signed the second statement received a month-long suspension from the college and the hospital. The decision also stipulated that students must withdraw their names from the statement, apologize, and agree to abide by the college bylaws in order to be readmitted to the university. Those who had signed only the first statement were allowed to return in a month's time without an apology.

The decision came into effect immediately. Students were barred from accessing their dorm rooms, from eating at the university cafeteria, and even from being on campus at the university and hospital.

The strikes had failed. The students hadn't achieved any of their demands, and each of them now had to sort out their affairs as they saw fit. Some of them refused to apologize and declare their submission, including students in their fourth and final year. They had to complete their studies at Cornelius van Dyck's home, with his help and guidance. Instead of receiving a university degree, they were granted a diploma from a medical committee established in Beirut that oversaw their exams, headed by Murad Bek, the Ottoman army doctor in the city. Istanbul accepted this document and allowed students holding it to take the licensing exam.

Students in the first three years who refused to apologize, however, were at an impasse. After losing hope of finding another way to continue their studies, most of them ended up returning to the college, apologizing in writing for what they had done, and pledging to observe the college's bylaws.

There were very few students, as it happened, who never apologized or came back, among whom were Jurji Zaidan, Hassan Nassar, and Amin Fleihan. Fares, meanwhile, didn't have to make an apology to be readmitted to the college because he didn't sign the December 16 statement, on the basis of which the administration had imposed these conditions. Despite that, he made the pivotal decision not to return and to find another way to complete his education. He saw it as an unquestionable matter of personal and national dignity.

Jurji Zaidan's position was more precarious than the other students; he was poorer than the rest, and his parents were unable to assist him. After careful consideration and consultation, Jurij therefore decided to move to Cairo to finish his studies at Qasr El Eyni, a well-known medical school at the time. What encouraged him to make the decision was that the *khawája* Melhem Shakour, from the village of Ayn Zhalta, was living in Cairo where he was president of the English schools in Faggala.[1] Amin Fleihan, who also hailed from Ayn Zhalta, wrote to Melhem and asked him about the possibility of coming to Cairo with his friend Jurji to complete their degrees. Melhem responded that if they came, they'd be accepted and enrolled in the appropriate classes. So Jurji and Amin made up their minds to travel and began requesting letters of recommendation from prestigious institutions in Beirut, Mount Lebanon, and Damascus.

Jurji went to Damascus and returned with a letter of recommendation from the Ottoman Fifth Army addressed to the president of Qasr El Eyni in Cairo, as well as a recommendation from the patriarch of Antioch addressed to the patriarch of Alexandria. He tried to obtain a letter from the wali of Damascus to the Egyptian Khedivate but was unsuccessful.[2] The wali declined, claiming he had no diplomatic ties with the Khedive. The real reason was that he didn't want to embarrass the American missionaries, given that his superior in Istanbul had a strong relationship with the United States consulate there (and would later appoint an Ottoman officer to accompany the American army to Cuba and learn from their combat strategies when the Spanish-American War erupted in 1898).

Amin Fleihan managed to obtain a letter of recommendation from the Mutasarrif of Mount Lebanon, Rüstem Pasha, to the Khedive of Egypt. The letter noted that the people of Greater Syria have had the right to attend Qasr El Eyni free of charge ever since Ibrahim Pasha's decade-long occupation of Beirut (describing it as a "visit" instead of an "occupation"), which ended only after the British fleet bombed Istanbul.

Jurji Zaidan borrowed a sum of money to complete his preparations for travel. His neighbor Omar al-Mahmasani, owner of a nuts and confectionery shop, loaned him six pounds.

1. In the Ottoman Empire, it was common to call prominent Christian merchants *khawája*, a Persian loanword (via Turkish) meaning "lord," distinguishing them from titles held predominantly by Muslims like *effendi, bey, pasha*.

2. A semiautonomous province of the Ottoman Empire, established in 1867 when Sultan Abdülaziz (r. 1861–78) granted Ismail Pasha (r. 1863–79) the title of *khedive* (Turkish *hidiv*, Arabic *khidéwi*), replacing the earlier title of *wáli* (governor) and recognizing Egypt's expanded autonomy within the empire.

"If this isn't enough," he told Jurji, "I'll give you more."

Fares had a different plan. He contacted his father, who was well informed about the progress of the strike, and brought up the idea of him coming to New York. Mansour was proud that his son had refused to comply with the administration, because he believed that no apology was necessary when dignity was concerned, no matter the cost. He also talked to other expatriates about the possibility of forming committees to contact the board of trustees in New York in support of the students.

The father eventually agreed to let Fares come to New York and complete his studies, albeit reluctantly—having underestimated the difficulty of the process himself, Mansour now knew that this decision would come at a great cost. Fares began preparing himself for the journey, first by asking professors with whom he was on good terms for recommendation letters. He also asked some moderate missionaries who had remained neutral during the dispute, and they met his requests without hesitation.

At this point, the paths of Fares Hashem and his lifelong companion Jurji Zaidan had begun to diverge. Still, they decided to travel to Alexandria with Amin, on the same day and on the same ship. This way, they could spend some time together before Fares continued his journey to New York.

The three of them set sail for Egypt in October 1883, the year after the Urabi revolt. At the time, Egypt had been struck by a cholera outbreak that claimed a harrowing number of lives, so they waited until the infections subsided before boarding an English merchant ship: the first vessel to carry passengers to Egypt since the epidemic.

None of the three had ever traveled by sea before or knew how to swim. They were aware that migration out of Mount Lebanon was rampant, but now they were experiencing it firsthand, alongside the hundreds of fellow migrants on board. Most of them had never laid eyes on the sea in their lives, much less traveled by ship, so they began making jokes about it in their own way. One of them hoped the sea would turn out to be a field in which to grow potatoes (which had reached Greater Syria relatively recently: First grown in the village of Ehden when the Protestant missionary Isaac Bird brought it over in 1827, the potato soon took hold across the entire region). Some travelers hoped the sea was made of olive oil for them to eat *kibbeh nayyeh*—ground lamb tartare with bulgur. Others dreamt it was full of fresh water they could use to irrigate all their rain-fed crops.

These mountain dwellers were astounded by the vastness of the sea. Realizing that not a person in the world could possibly pave over all of it, they came up with the phrase *bállit al-báhr*—"Go pave the sea!"—meaning that you're unable to meet the challenge before you.

Jurji concluded that it had been the provincial immigrants who coined the idiom, an observation that prompted a deep discussion on the present and future of the Arabic language. All expressed confidence that the language would be able to overcome the past five centuries of stagnation. After all, its people were rising up, and many had begun traversing the seas and exploring the world to amass the treasures of advanced civilizations, accruing wealth and all kinds of wisdom to bring home for their countries to turn to their advantage.

The debate about the Arabic language and its relevance to the modern era was a heated one within all intellectual circles, particularly in schools and universities established by Jesuit and Protestant missionaries, as well as in the burgeoning field of print journalism.

Advocates of the Arabic language were multiplying at an astonishing pace in both Christian and Muslim communities. The printing presses were beginning to flourish, and Beirut was on its way to becoming the publishing capital of the East.

What register should be used? What vocabulary? What syntax? What style? The written language had been wasting away on bookshelves for centuries. If it weren't for the authority of the Quran in the hearts of Arabs—both Muslims and Christians, ordinary people and the literary vanguard—then Arabic would have died out and been replaced by Turkish, the language of the Ottoman Empire.

Unsurprisingly, it was the expression "Go pave the sea" that gave rise to this linguistic conversation. At the time, mastery of language and literature was part of a physician's specialization. The three of them were aware that Mr. Boutros al-Boustani had discussed the matter at length and in detail with the famous *Nahdawi* poet Nasif al-Yaziji and the American missionary Eli Smith. Smith had served as head of the committee tasked with translating the Bible until his death in 1859, when he was succeeded by Cornelius van Dyck. The committee decided to simplify the language, to translate using a form of Arabic that was refined yet simultaneously accessible.

*Pay attention, Fares!*

Fares was aware of this discussion about Arabic, the language he adored. Its revival, to him, was the revival of his nation and himself.

*Fares!*

A voice was calling out to him.

*The Arabic language shall prevail!*

His professors at the college used to promote this disposition to every student, for various reasons. First, Arabic was the language of the Quran and the people. The Ottoman Empire was on the verge of dissolution in the eyes of the West, and advocating for Arabic was a step in that direction. Further, this was the age of nationalism, and nationalist ideologies were at their zenith, especially in Europe and America. Many Syrian and Arab intellectuals and elites adopted these concepts across all disciplines. They saw the Arabic language as a great source of national unity: a weapon that the Turkish language could not withstand.

The three young men were proficient in Arabic, Turkish, French, and English. All of them were dressed in the "Western" way—slacks, a shirt, and a jacket—save for their heads, on which they each wore a red Ottoman fez. So strongly did they resemble foreigners that the owner of the small boat they rode from the dock of the bay to the ship initially tried to communicate with them using the few words from European languages he'd picked up from his interactions with foreign visitors, because it was uncommon to see someone wearing European clothes. Most parents forbade their children from wearing Western clothing instead of Ottoman garb, because the former would invite nosiness and mockery from most people. The few families that had the audacity to allow this stark deviation did so very reluctantly.

Unfortunately, the steamship they had to ride was full of livestock. The smell was unbearable, so they spent their time on deck. Bewildered and frustrated, they were unsure of how to let the agent from whom they'd purchased their tickets know about this. He had promised them a luxurious ferry, that most passengers aboard would be Europeans, and that they would *essentially* be in first class in terms of the quality of service and the fresh, tasty food. Based on what they'd heard, they were eager to pay the amount requested at the time. Fares covered part of the cost of a ticket for Jurji, who initially declined the offer, until Fares made him swear on their friendship.

The travel agent's scam prompted a conversation, amid their astonishment, about dishonesty in Greater Syria. There were American missionaries who didn't hide their opinion of the country's people. Some of them had written about how lying was a fundamental part of being Syrian. At the college, some of their professors articulated this view openly in class: especially Dr. Post, who they voiced their grievances against by name to the board of trustees during the strikes.

# 14

"Don't be like others from your country," Dr. Post used to say. He frequently told them about the problems he encountered with merchants of all kinds. He wasn't used to bargaining over prices: In America, they were fixed and no one haggled. But here, whenever Post went to the market to buy something, he'd return angry, muttering something a missionary once wrote: "Dishonesty is endemic to these people, as much a biological necessity as water and oxygen. Merchants don't tell the truth, nor do laborers, blacksmiths, carpenters, builders, or tailors—none of them do."

Dr. Post would tell his students that sincerity—in word and deed—is the surest mark of faith. But it seemed like what he really wanted was for them to follow Christ above all else. His students, on the other hand, wanted to be recognized as citizens first, believing that genuine faith could only come from genuine citizenship. In fact, this is not far from what Dr. Post and many of their American colleagues, like the president of the university, Dr. Bliss, believed in as well: but only for their own kind.

To be a real American, you had to be a true Christian. And to be a true Christian, of course, you had to be Protestant!

The three drifted into endless banter, trading stories about their countrymen—how they never told the truth, never kept a promise, never showed up when they said they would.

"Even my mother used to lie!" Fares burst out suddenly, with anger. Then, all at once, he broke down sobbing uncontrollably before everyone on the deck.

Jurji and Amin stood in front of him teary-eyed, watching him as if he were crying not only for himself but for them too.

It hadn't even been a year since Imm Fares had died, and he was telling them that she used to lie. One day, he told them, a European man spent the night at their neighbor's house and left his saddlebag outside, in which he had forgotten his watch. Watches were luxury items at the time. But when the man woke up the next morning, he couldn't find it. Fares was sure it had been his mother who stole the foreigner's watch because he later found out that she went to see a watch seller and sold it to him. This was after they had stopped receiving news from Fares's father.

"What one does in desperate times can't be considered dishonesty!" Jurji argued.

"Of course it can!" Fares replied. He told Jurji that when the neighbors came to ask his mother about the missing watch, he watched as she fervently denied having anything to do with it. She swore by the Lord God, Jesus Christ, and the Virgin Mary that she hadn't seen it or touched it, that she never went near the saddlebag.

"Our parents teach us to lie from a young age," Fares surmised. "My mother used to tell me and my siblings when we were young that if we didn't go to sleep, a wolf would eat us."

From the upper deck of the ship, he shouted toward the shore—toward Beirut, toward the neighborhood where they once lived.

"What wolf, *Ímmi*?!" he hurled at the top of his lungs. "The wolf didn't eat us—the sea did! Look at me now, getting swallowed up by the same sea that took *Bába* years ago. And you—you were taken by the earth, and now you're finally at eternal peace."

But Fares didn't consider himself a migrant. He was a student, traveling to finish his studies in New York—where his father lived—only to then return to his country and forge his future there, contributing to its renaissance.

The same was true for Jurji Zaidan, who had no idea at the time about the illustrious place he would one day take up in Arab intellectual history.

When Fares snapped himself out of his outburst, wiping his tears from his nose and his eyes until they cleared again, he observed his friends crying quietly, like him. He saw the passengers standing in the same area as them, turning away from them. Fares then approached his friends.

"Let's take an oath that we'll return to our country after we finish our studies," Fares whispered to his friends. "*Yálla*—repeat after me!"

The friends switched from speaking in their usual colloquial dialect to classical Arabic. Now the conversation had become solemn, the moment fateful.

"I swear to God Almighty," Fares began in a clear yet stifled voice, "that, upon my graduation, I shall return to my blessed country, that I shall take part in its rebirth in all its cities and each of its unspoiled villages."

Jurji and Amin repeated after him in the same forceful yet hushed tone so as not to alert anyone on the ship, especially since the customs officer had come to the ship's deck to verify the "legality" of the passengers' papers.

This was the third time that customs officers inspected the passengers' papers. The first was when they passed the customs building. Each of them had paid half a *majidiyya*—worth one-fifth of an Ottoman lira—that they slipped underneath their passports before presenting them to the officer on duty.[1] The second time their papers were inspected, they were on the small boat that ferried them from the wharf to the ship. They did the same thing as before: An officer asked for their passports—and, this time, for a whole *majidiyya*. And there they were again, for the third time, handing over their passports and money . . . all so the officer could verify that everything was above board!

They had thought that they would be able to avoid paying the *bakhshísh* once they had reached the ship's deck as an act of resistance against the rampant corruption plaguing the Ottoman administration and society.[2] But one of the captain's officers who knew the Port of Beirut well and didn't want a problem to arise warned them that not paying could be risky. The officer who boarded the boat could easily prevent the ship from setting to sea, or send them back to land—even if his behavior was illegal.

1. In addition to the *majidíyya* (Turkish *mecidiye*), the Ottoman lira at the time was divided into one hundred piastres (*kuruş*) and four thousand *paras*.

2. A sum of money paid to facilitate an official transaction, akin to a tip or an outright bribe; also spelled *baksheesh*.

Jurji and Amin burst into tears as the ship sailed away from the port. As Beirut receded farther and farther in the distance, they recalled why they were doing what they were doing. They started talking about the benefits of immigration for the sake of the nation's rebirth.

Those two would continue their studies at Qasr El Eyni in Cairo. Then they would return to Beirut—God permitting!—to carry out their patriotic responsibilities to their people. Their efforts would benefit the nation even if they went on to find work in Egypt—the land of the Nile and al-Mu'izz's Cairo.[3]

3. The city of Cairo was founded by the Fatimid Empire in 969 under the fourth caliph al-Mu'izz li-Din Allah (r. 953–75). The Arabic name Cairo (*al-Qáhira*), still in use today, derives from the formal title "the Victorious City of al-Mu'izz" (*al-Qáhira al-Mu'izzíyya*).

# 15

Fares, on the other hand, still had a long way to go.

But it was America!

He swore to his friends that he'd try his best to finish his studies without wasting any time, while also absorbing as much of the culture as possible, learning civic virtues and all the attributes of civilized men along the way. This would especially include learning how to love one's country. And he swore that he would return to Lebanon after completing these tasks.

They were in agreement. "Migration—which implies getting acquainted with and absorbing modernity in all its forms—will enrich the beneficial parts of our heritage that befit the era. This encounter with modernity will birth a future civilization. There's no other way. We shouldn't cry, then. We should rejoice: We're taking a critical step toward renewing the nation."

Upon disembarking from the ship at the port of Alexandria, they were greeted by a representative of Melhem Bek Shakour. Melhem Bek took care of them, making sure Jurji and Amin had food and a place to lodge for a few days before the two went to Cairo. For three days they wandered the streets of Alexandria, visiting its cultural monuments and appreciating the rebirth that the country was undergoing in full swing.

Melhem took care of them, because they were from the country. Amin hailed from Melhem's village of Ayn Zhalta, and he was also a Protestant. What's more, their families survived the massacre in Deir al-Qamar together, having fled there from Ayn Zhalta. They hid in the basement of Bird, the Protestant missionary. It was a moment that strengthened the friendship and bond between the two families.

Then the group split up. Jurji and Amin continued their journey to Cairo, and Fares spent several more days in Alexandria awaiting the arrival of the French ship *Grandeur.* The ship, on its way from Beirut, was bound for Marseille, France.

Fares felt lonely when the ship was delayed. He began to visit the site of the famous Pharos lighthouse, erected by Alexander the Great, several times a day. The place brought to mind flashbacks of the stories and legends that he'd read about its construction. In particular, he remembered the story of how sea creatures would emerge from the water every night only to destroy what the builders had accomplished during the day. Alexander ordered a large case to be lowered to the bottom of the sea. He descended into it along with two artists. Once they reached the ocean's depths, the artists sketched the creatures from inside the case. Upon their return, Alexander had sculptures of the creatures made so that when they came back out at night, they would flee at the sight of their own likenesses and never return.

As he contemplated the effects of time on human civilization, Fares wished he could compose a poem—but he was no poet.

The sea in Alexandria deepened his sense that a national renaissance, a *náhda,* must occur. The Arabs must awaken from their slumber. The words of the *Nahdawi* poet Nasif al-Yaziji came to his mind, so he stood before the sea and, as if standing before an audience, began to recite:

تنبَّهوا واستفيقوا أيُّها العرب!

*Awaken, O Arabs, and take heed!*

But he felt an overwhelming sense of loneliness that grew stronger within him until it nearly overcame him—so he sought guidance.

A woman is the best companion to a man who feels alienated and far from his family and homeland—and Fares had a natural predilection for women. He had enough money to stay in good hotels and meet women from the upper class. His father had sent him a sum that allowed for such a lifestyle, and he had also saved from various jobs he took on, such as translation, private tutoring, and the like.

Fares had not imagined just how expensive it would be to specialize in medicine in America, so he spent what he had frivolously.

At night he would visit a lady named Bilat who would serve him the most delicious food. When he finished his meal, she would wash his hands and dry them for him. She'd drape a towel over her open palms, as if in prayer, then fill it with water and wipe them off. Then she'd serve him the most sophisticated French wine—the very wine her friend, the descendant of one of Napoleon's high-ranking officers, used to drink. He had remained in Egypt after the French army's withdrawal in 1802, married an Egyptian woman, and become fully Egyptian—trading in cotton, buying steamships, and leaving behind an inheritance of companies and properties to his children and grandchildren.

Fares was astonished when Bilat told him that she was completely happy with her work and had chosen this profession of her own accord! But why should she be forced to choose a profession at all?

*Who, in our countries, would force women to work?* Fares thought to himself. *A woman's parents are supposed to look after her until she gets married.*

Fares had never heard of a woman taking up this profession of her own accord—much less being proud of it! When he tried to ask her about her family, she refused, objecting that they'd prefer not to be her parents.

"I love them," she said, "but I wouldn't want them to be my parents because it would torment them to death . . . to the point of being killed. That's why they don't know anything about me, and I don't know anything about them. All I know is that they live in Cairo and even that I wish I didn't know.

"If they saw me now they wouldn't recognize me because I've changed so much physically—I've gained a lot of weight compared to how I looked when I was with them. Then I scratched myself just above my eyebrows to distort my face, so no one would recognize me. I always dye my hair blonde, though my real hair is pitch black. See this tooth? I had it capped with gold even though it's healthy."

All of this she revealed to Fares, now that she'd come to trust him and had grown attached. Bilat liked Fares. Fares liked her, too. But her insistence that she had chosen this profession of her own accord bothered him deeply—frightened him, even. It shook his sense of balance the first time she told him. How in the world could a woman enjoy this profession?

Women are forced to do this; life's hardship drives them to it. What sane woman would choose to make her living by sleeping with a different man every day—sometimes every hour?

The prostitute whom he'd grown fond of in Beirut—Yorma—used to bawl from the depths of her soul when she told him about the circumstances that pushed her into this humiliating profession.

Yorma wasn't proud of her line of work. On the contrary, she was ashamed of it in the deepest, most intense way and perpetually tried to rid herself of it. To Fares, this was natural to see. But Bilat in Alexandria was the total opposite. She took pride in her work, and she enjoyed it. If she didn't fear retaliation from all of society, she'd have spoken openly about what she did. She'd have written about it in newspapers and magazines. But the year was 1883, and the city was Alexandria.

Bilat occupied Fares's thoughts. He thought of her constantly, day and night, to such an extent that sleep eluded him for days on end. He would abruptly get out of bed and head back toward her place, already having spent his evening there. One time she told him not to come over in the afternoon because her friend, the French officer's grandson, had returned from Cairo and would stay in Alexandria for several days. She said he could see her in the morning before noon if he wanted to.

But he didn't go see her before noon—not in the afternoon or in the following days, either. Yet Bilat would forever stay in his memory as a riddle he would never crack: a woman who chose to work as a prostitute because she loved it!

# 16

As the ship began to drift away from the port of Alexandria, Fares noticed that a sort of exile from the country had begun in earnest. He felt his eyes well up. He could no longer swallow his saliva. He'd never before experienced such a condition but recalled that it had a name. It was a *ghússa*—a lump in the throat!

What hurt him most deeply was the sight of those children, the children of his country, accompanying their parents or relatives, suffering from seasickness. They swayed and doubled over—complexions pallid, bodies contorted—atop a solid surface surrounded by great, rugged waters extending into the distance. They were completely unaware of where they were, what was happening, or why. All they knew was what their families had told them: "We're going to America. We'll stay there for a few years, then we'll come back. We'll build houses, we'll start businesses that we can live off."

They were told that the trip would take two months, most of it by sea and a bit by land. They'd pass through France by train, from the city of Marseille on the Mediterranean to Le Havre on the Atlantic.

The train consisted of large boxes with glass openings that pulled themselves, without need for animals or men. They were affixed to large iron wheels, shaped like sieves, that rolled along two strips of iron that they call "tracks." A train could pick up mountains and move them somewhere else without feeling pain or fatigue—as it had no soul.

Only souls get tired! That's why those children felt tired.

Only souls feel pain! That's why those children felt pain.

"These are the children of my country!" Fares remarked.

He felt the desire to sing folk songs, songs of parting—something like what Wadih El-Safi used to perform in recent times, with lyrics composed by Assad Elsebaali:

يا مهاجرين ارجعوا
غالي الوطن غالي

*O migrants, come back!*
*How dear the homeland is—how precious!*[1]

But he held back. To cry in that moment would have been at odds with his conviction that in the lands of Syria a new kind of humanity must be created, that a new breed of citizens, who follow their reason and intellect, not emotions and impulse—citizens committed to the renaissance of their people, to the right of the nation to live in dignity—must emerge. This nation had to be steadfast amid the fray of warfare, resolute in the face of howling gales: a united nation that rises up as one amid tempestuous seas, that will have a pioneering role to play in the worldwide race toward glory.

So Fares stopped himself from crying, vowing to agonize for the sake of the nation's renaissance instead.

Once they were at sea, he realized that all he could see was sky and water. An irrational fear swept through him: The sky was clear and the sea was eerily calm. As he stood on the ship's edge, leaning on the railing and peering out at the deep and mysterious sea, he sensed fear overtaking him. Fares felt an enchanting presence in the bottom of the sea calling out to him. Afraid that he'd answer the call, he suddenly backed away. He sat on the floor to keep the call from tempting him, lest it lead him to his demise, to hurling himself overboard into that mystery.

But the weather didn't remain clear for the entirety of the journey. Halfway through, it transformed without warning into a tempest. Winds and waves flung the ship back and forth so violently that not a single person

1. Wadih El-Safi (1921–2013) was a Lebanese tenor, composer, and cultural icon. He recorded many songs written by Assaad Elsebaali (1910–1999), a Lebanese pioneer of *zájal* (colloquial) poetry celebrating themes of rural life.

went unperturbed. Many of them got sick and vomited—some furtively, others tactfully, and still others overtly.

It occurred to Fares that man is a fragile creature—that the two natural elements surrounding them, water and wind, were numb to the discomforts of life at sea. The elements have neither friend nor foe. When the sea is in a state of agitation, it's not because it's angry or vengeful. And when the sea is calm, it's not because it's loving and merciful. He had thrown up everything that was inside of him and still the tempest continued to rock the ship.

The water began increasing until it reached the ship's deck, making him think that he was in the depths of the sea and not on its surface. But the storm didn't last long, quieting in less than two days, and Fares began to regain his morale.

In spite of everything, Fares would not let himself regret the sacrifice he was making by traveling far away to study. It was all part of the plan to return to his country and contribute to its renaissance with all his might.

The first step that Fares took when the ship moored at the port of Marseille—after disembarking, getting his documents checked, and passing the health inspection—was to throw off his red Ottoman fez and buy a top hat. He then took off with the friends he'd met on the ship to explore the city, all of them mesmerized amid the glow of the electric lights that illuminated the homes, streets, and public spaces.

Fares and his friends stood under an electric streetlight and began to whirl around the way someone taking a shower sways under the showerhead.

"If only I were a poet!" Fares repeated several times. "I'm bathing in light!" he shouted. Years later his compatriot, Gibran Khalil Gibran, would say in his famous poem "Give Me the Flute and Sing":

هل تحمَّمتَ بعِطرٍ
وتنشَّفتَ بنورٍ؟
وشربتَ الفجرَ خمرًا
في كؤوسٍ من أثيرٍ؟

*Have you ever bathed in perfume*
*and dried yourself with light?*

*Have you ever drunk dawn, like wine,*
*from chalices of morning's breeze?*[2]

"When will Beirut bask in the brilliance of these lights?" Fares mused. "When will they reach the villages of Lebanon's proud, lofty mountains . . . or all of Syria's cities, towns, and hamlets, for that matter? When will light replace darkness?"

He repeatedly strained his neck from staring up at the multistory buildings and counting their floors one by one. The buildings were laid out in a predetermined pattern from which none could deviate.

*Country of mine, when will the time come?*

2. Gibran Khalil Gibran (1883–1931) was a Lebanese American poet and artist, author of *The Prophet*, and a prominent voice of the *Mahjar*, an early twentieth-century literary movement of Arab immigrants to the Americas.

# 17

Fares was astonished by the paved streets for vehicles, juxtaposed with sidewalks for pedestrians—men as well as women! The women walked alone: unperturbed, undaunted, and unaccompanied by men.

Fares knew French fairly well, which facilitated his ability to find the brothels. He was joined by a young man from northern Lebanon whom he had met at the hotel and whose company he had come to enjoy. His name was Rashid. Rashid was planning to join his relatives and siblings in Puerto Rico, where he would later die. Several years later, he caught syphilis from the large number of prostitutes he had slept with without protection or discretion. When Fares learned of his death, he wrote a letter to Rashid's siblings to offer his condolences. He bemoaned the ignorance of the time and Rashid's alienation from his homeland.

But Fares was extremely prudent when sleeping with prostitutes. His medical knowledge helped him to be so. He didn't dare do everything he wanted to. He prioritized what he was able to do over what he dreamt of doing. His principle: as much pleasure and as little risk as possible.

Once he met a prostitute who didn't know French very well so he asked her, in Arabic, if she was from Mount Lebanon. She replied in broken French that she was from Spain. He looked at her in astonishment.

"So how in the world did you understand my question?"

She panicked and ran away, leaving him naked in the room. She must've been from Mount Lebanon, or from one of the villages or towns in Greater Syria.

"Poverty, hardship, ignorance!" Fares sighed. He wanted to know more about that woman, but she was gone.

The journey to Paris was by rail. Fares was dumbstruck by the train with its iron cars slinking through the streets like a snake, passing the city squares and the fields in the countryside.

The smoke billowing from the locomotive's smokestacks resembled a salute, a bright indication that reason would triumph over ignorance and tradition. It dispersed into the air like a grin, like a sign that victory was night and hope smiled upon the future with brightness and clarity.

The train's whistle made Fares feel as if he could fly. In his euphoria he felt lightweight, as though he could soar like a bird. This was long before the invention of the airplane would appear on the horizon.

But he also felt a sort of despondency as the train traversed the countless identical plains under gray skies. The sun seemed to him like a gift from the sky as it periodically peeked out over the world, illuminating those wide-open spaces.

Fares wished he could stay in Paris longer, but he was worried that the ship, *L'Atlantique,* would arrive and depart from Le Havre before he could make it.

He managed to walk around for a few hours through the neighborhoods surrounding the station. He was amazed by the wide, straight boulevards—but what most captured his attention was people's clothing.

Men and women dressed in elegant, clean suits. He sensed in them a pride in something that he was unable to identify. This pride he deduced from their attire, the way they walked, and the way they spoke to one another. One man called another *monsieur,* "my lord"—*sídi* in Arabic—no matter how humble his interlocutor's status.

Everyone was in a big hurry in Paris. Fares noticed he hadn't seen a single person—man or woman—standing on the sidewalk and passing time without a reason.

"Where are they going in such a hurry?" Fares wondered to himself.

His companion, Rashid, didn't understand anything he was seeing. It was like he lived in a world of vague illusions, a world of dust. It resembled our world, just as God alone perceived it prior to its creation—but with a tint. Rashid couldn't see or hear well. He was floating someplace without gravity to pull him in any particular direction.

But Fares was aware of his surroundings and what was happening around him. He knew especially well that he was in a land civilized and developed, sophisticated and free.

Suddenly the two heard a rumbling sound, like the roar of crashing waves, growing closer. They panicked and began making their way back to the station, where they'd be safe. But the streets had filled up with overlapping throngs of countless people, marching and shouting, waving cloth banners bearing written messages, their fists held high with rage.

Then the two of them suddenly heard a roaring sound approaching, like the crashing of waves, and they panicked. While on their return to the train station to find safety from a potential danger, they crossed an immeasurable number of humans. People gathered in close proximity, marching, shouting, carrying signs, raising their fists.

"Workers!" Fares said to Rashid, in an attempt to mitigate his worries. But the word did nothing to calm Rashid's unease.

"What?"

"They're workers! Workers!" Fares replied. "Supporters of Darwin!" he added with overwhelming joy.

Fares set aside the memory of Darwin as he explained to Rashid what "workers" meant, how they work and where, how they organize themselves into what they call "unions" and demand something called "rights." He explained how most of them don't really believe in religion, that some demand to be ruled by one of their own, that they openly despise kings and monarchs. Rashid grew scared and felt he'd lost his balance. Every certainty had been shaken. He wanted to go back to his village.

At the port of Le Havre, Fares purchased a first-class ticket at quite a high price—not only for his comfort, but for a greater reason. He wanted to give a good impression that his country was not only a land of poor, wretched people. No—there were many people who aspired to greatness, who wished to live as foreigners did, or even better.

At the travel office, Fares astonished the clerk with his elegant and precise French. He'd absorbed it from reading books at the schools where he studied in Beirut. It was only natural to the clerk that Fares should travel first class, considering the expertise he'd acquired in a language other than his native tongue.

"Where did you learn French?" the clerk asked him, impressed.

"In Beirut," Fares replied, then added: "At school!"

He added that detail so the French clerk understood that there were important schools in Beirut where people learned languages to the point of mastery.

"I love the French language," Fares added, "because it's the language of the revolutionaries, the language of Robespierre, the orator of the great revolution who told the king's messenger: 'We are here by the will of the people, and only by the power of bayonets shall we depart!'"

"You know this, too!" the clerk exclaimed, nearly leaping up and kissing him. Straightaway, he proposed that Fares attend an instructional meeting of the socialist association he was a member of, stressing that this association was international, not nationalist. Instead of answering the question, Fares asked the clerk whether he supported Darwin's theory.

"Who's Darwin?" the man replied.

Fares was taken aback by the fact that this clerk, a self-declared international socialist, didn't know who Darwin was. How could such a person be ignorant of Darwin? Fares thanked him for the invitation, telling himself that Syrians ought to look after their own first before concerning themselves with the world at large.

"We'll meet soon, alongside the other nations!" Fares told the clerk, who didn't understand what he meant.

But the real problem came when the American ticket inspector refused to let Fares travel in first class alongside the other tall, white, blond-haired, blue-eyed passengers.

Fares was of average height, with honey-colored eyes and olive skin. But they wouldn't accept him in first class.

The American, uncompromising in his refusal, insisted that Fares travel in third class with the rest of the Syrians, despite the ticket he carried. Fares, however, insisted on first class, seeing this rejection as a denial of his country's right to sit at the table of nations. He tried to slip past the inspector, but the man shoved him with such force that he knocked him overboard!

As Fares plunged into the Atlantic, he didn't feel afraid— he was livid. But once he was truly submerged, he began to panic because he couldn't swim well. He became convinced he was going to drown.

At the same time, however, he grew excited by the thought of dying as a martyr for his country—right in front of the other Syrian travelers, who were witnessing what was happening. As he began to drown he felt a sort of happiness and contentment, despite being in great distress. His countrymen could see him drowning, and they knew why. They'd tell everyone back home and in their new destinations what they were seeing with their own eyes. They'd honor him as a martyr who died for his country's independence. They'd see him as a beacon that lit the way toward progress. As he sank, he wished he were able to tell them, "Bury me in my country, so my blood might fertilize the soil and make it sprout bright red flowers every spring."

But there were small boats surrounding the Leviathan American ship, which swiftly rescued him and brought him ashore before he could swallow too much water and drown. His people gathered around him—most importantly, his friend Rashid—and took care of him. Since there was still ample time before the ship set sail, he went to the market and bought new clothes.

Fares purchased expensive, elegant clothing—the latest in men's fashion in France. He visited the Frenchman who'd sold him the ticket and told him what had happened. Enraged at what he was hearing, the man assured him that the French constitution prohibits discrimination and treats all people as citizens with equal rights and duties. So long as Fares was in French territorial waters, this American had no right to stop him from doing as he pleased. The man sent for the port police and informed them of the situation. They took action and questioned the inspector, who denied having intentionally knocked Fares into the water. He claimed he only meant to prevent Fares from accessing the first-class cabin. They took issue with his excuse and informed him that his behavior was in violation of French law.

And so fate had it that Fares became the first Syrian, the first Easterner, to travel first class to America. He'd paved the way, and others would follow. Before, all people coming from the Eastern Mediterranean were forced to travel third class, in cramped cabins like crates, below deck, or in lounges overflowing with other travelers heading to America: mostly migrants from the poorest parts of Europe and from across the Ottoman Empire. They were crammed together like cattle and slept on top of one another amid the stench of waste, coal smoke, and bodies unwashed since birth.

Fares's friend Rashid, for example, had never washed his entire body in his life. He used to wash only his hair once a month, maybe less. People in those days were afraid of bathing, as it was widely believed to cause deadly diseases.

Fares had a good time in first class. He had a compartment to himself, and the food was clean and delicious—unlike that of his friend Rashid and his countrymen.

Some of them, despite their hunger, routinely turned down meals because the food was tasteless. The gruel was served in buckets and pans. Each person was served a portion in a small, shallow bowl. As a result, they relied on the dried foods they had brought: figs, olives, jerky, and balls of *shanklísh* and *lábneh*. They would reach into their bags and nibble on small amounts when they felt very hungry—or when they wanted to feel connected to their homeland.

Fares may have been riding first class, but his heart and mind were in steerage, where his people languished in the most squalid conditions. He visited them often and would also encounter them on the ship's deck when they were allowed to come up. Once, Fares joined Rashid up there for an impromptu dinner of olives, a small ball of dried *lábneh*, and a piece of *shanklísh*. Rashid sat cross-legged at the bow and poured them each a glass of *arak* on that clear evening, and they drank a toast to their country. Then Rashid began to sing traditional ballads of separation and longing in his beautiful, wounded voice. As they sat there, the two suddenly caught sight of a young Syrian woman as she exited a sailor's cabin, made her way to the edge of the ship, threw up, then slipped away out of embarrassment.

Then the ocean started playing around—and the ship, too! The vessel began to thrash to and fro, before they could even finish their *arak*. Rashid, in his Mount Lebanon accent, called out to the ocean:

"Are you playing tough, O Atlantic?" he reproached.

Rashid realized that this could be the opening line of a *zájal*—a kind of oral poem in colloquial Arabic. He considered adding to it but felt incapable, particularly as the boat had sailed into the storm's more turbulent depths.

Seventy years later, that very line would resurface, woven into the opening verse of a poem by the famous Lebanese *zájal* poet Tanious Hemlawe.[1] With a glass of *arak* in hand, he stood on the deck of a ship slicing through the vast Atlantic, bound for America. As the ocean rocked the vessel, his glass trembled and spilled, prompting Tanious to raise his voice and address the restless sea:

عم تتمرجل يا طلنتيك
والحملاوي مسافر فيك؟
إن الله وصّلني ع الشطّ
وانقرت الدفّ بفرجيك!

*Are you playing tough, O Atlantic,*
*as Hemlawe makes his way across you?!*
*As soon as God gets me to shore,*
*when the drum beats, I'll show you!*

Had Tanious caught wind of Rashid's turn of phrase and his desire to turn it into verse? Or perhaps Rashid was one of the many Lebanese mountain villagers who crossed the ocean without ever having seen the sea before, whom the sea provoked and taunted, who felt impotent before it and accused it of coming after unarmed men, nursing mothers, and helpless children—hardly a feat of manliness! Does the sea don a cloak of masculinity simply because it is a route that travelers must take toward their far-flung destination—America? Why would it roil and churn beneath them as they traveled across it, just wanting to be safe, not meaning any harm?

Later on, Hemlawe's words came to be considered some of the most beautiful verses of *zájal*.

Once the ocean settled after days of raging winds and heavy rain, Fares and Rashid regained their interest in the woman they'd seen come

1. Tanious Hemlawe (1912–1996), born in the village of Hemlaya, founded several choirs and edited *zájal*-focused magazines such as *al-Shuʻla* (1955–70).

out of the sailor's cabin to vomit. They observed her carefully, with a hint of hesitation, and inquired about her to find out who she was and what village she came from. She was on her way to reunite with her husband, who had migrated two years earlier, just days after their wedding.

He wrote to her constantly, his letters filled with longing, and sent back what little money he could even though his work and living conditions afforded him little and didn't allow for her to join him. But now his circumstances had improved and he'd started living on his own in a small room near Washington Street in New York.

She was full-figured without being overweight, of average height, and had brownish, wheat-colored skin. She had come to be known simply as "the woman" in their conversations; they never mentioned her by name, as though it'd be a personal affront to do so. They talked a great deal about her situation.

Rashid's opinion was that it was wrong of her to visit the sailor in his cabin. Her actions tarnished not only her honor but that of her husband, her family, and all the Syrian travelers. Rashid wanted to hit her to put a stop to it. But Fares deterred him, reminding him that American laws were in force there aboard the ship and would apply to him if he struck her. And if she were to press charges against him, he'd go to prison.

"In America, women are free. They walk the streets unveiled, like we saw in Paris, Marseille, and Le Havre. They get drunk like men, they stagger through the streets like men. But the majority of them are honorable, and many are models of piety and refinement. They lead charitable organizations that support the needy and aid the distressed—keeping themselves far removed from anything that might detract from their reputation or bring dishonor upon themselves or their families.

"Women contribute the lion's share of the effort in elevating the stature of the nation—and in them the words of al-Mutanabbi ring true:

وَلَو كانَ النِّسَاءُ كَمَن فَقَدنا لَفُضِّلَتِ النِّسَاءُ عَلى الرِّجالِ
وَمَا التَّأنِيثُ لِاسْمِ الشَّمسِ عَيْبٌ وَلا التَّذكِيرُ فَخْرٌ لِلهِلالِ

*"If all women were like her whom we mourn,*
*then women would be better than men.*

*There is no shame in 'the sun' being a feminine noun,*
*nor may the moon take pride in being masculine."*[2]

"Do you know who al-Mutanabbi was, Rashid?" Fares asked.

Rashid shook his head, so Fares told him.

"Al-Mutanabbi is one of the most celebrated Arab poets. Some even say he's the greatest poet the Arabic language has ever known. This was a man who held himself so far above others that one day he declared:

الخَيلُ واللَّيلُ والبَيداءُ تَعرِفُني          والسَّيفُ والرُّمحُ والقِرطاسُ والقَلَمُ

*"The horses, the nights, the badlands know me well—*
*as do the sword and the spear, the parchment and the pen!"*

Fares had unwittingly entangled himself by reciting those lines. Rashid was illiterate: He couldn't tell the simple vertical stroke of the letter *álif* apart from the mast of a ship. He asked lots of questions until he could make sense of the verse. He had to ask Fares about the meaning of the words "badlands" and "parchment," about what the poet meant by saying they "know me." All of these questions Fares had to answer in order to get what he wanted: to introduce his illiterate countryman to one of the greatest poets of his Arabic language. He'd chosen this verse carefully, because it glorifies both bravery and intellect in a single breath.

"Then there's his name," Fares explained. "The poet is known as 'Mutanabbi' because he claimed to be a *nábi*—a prophet."

"Seriously?!" Rashid asked, astonished.

But Fares didn't respond. He was lost in thought—annoyed once again by the image of that young woman. His annoyance, as he told Rashid, was first and foremost patriotic: She'd given a bad impression of their homeland by acting the way she did. The sailors, the ship's crew, and the passengers of various nationalities might assume that all women from their

2. Abu al-Tayyib Ahmad al-Mutanabbi (915–965) was an Abbasid-era poet, celebrated for his eloquence, vivid praise of his eminent patrons, and self-assertive genius. These two verses come from an elegy the poet composed in memory of the mother of his patron Sayf al-Dawla al-Hamdani, emir of Aleppo (r. 945–67).

country were like her. Moreover, it suggested she was cheating on her immigrant husband who toiled day and night—enduring cold and heat, wandering through cities and across the countryside alone like a drifter, with no idea where he'd spend the night or whether rain or snow awaited him—all so he could provide his wife and children with a decent life and a bright future.

The suffering of the immigrants from Mount Lebanon and elsewhere in Ottoman Syria was widely known. It was common knowledge that the vast majority of them worked as peddlers and faced countless hardships: language barriers, ignorance of local customs, the weather's vicissitudes, discrimination due to their skin color and religion, and the long distances they traveled to sell the contents of the box they carried on their backs and hung around their necks, filled with combs, elastics, hairpins, shirt buttons, cufflinks, bobbins, threads, needles, scissors, hair trimmers, earrings, leather straps, bracelets, necklaces, and whatever else the distant and isolated housewives needed.

Peddling was harder for them than working in factories. But they still chose to do it, because it guaranteed them freedom that the factories did not . . . only for their wives to go out and cheat on them with strangers!

That was unacceptable.

Fares was disturbed, then, for patriotic as well as humanistic reasons. Had that woman been from one of the great, advanced nations, had her husband been well-to-do, he wouldn't have felt the way he did.

And he felt humiliated!

Poverty, hardship, and ignorance must be defeated! Fares had been right to endure the pains of travel. Everything in life entitled him to do so.

# 18

It didn't surprise Fares not to find his father waiting for him. There wasn't a single person from Mount Lebanon, nor anywhere else in Syria, among those waiting on the wharf. First-class passengers, most of whom were Americans, were simply treated differently. So, as Fares quickly made his way to shore, the other travelers from his country, and from all manner of other countries, had to proceed aboard another ferry to a place where papers would be checked and medical examinations would be conducted. They would spend long days there before being allowed to enter New York City.

Fares could have taken the streetcar from the port to where his father lived, but he preferred to hire his own carriage so he wouldn't have to trouble himself with lugging his things on and off the streetcar like his countrymen. He'd committed the address to memory and didn't need to double check it in the notebook where he had written it down.

When Fares reached the house, his father wasn't there. He realized his father may have spent long hours at the port waiting for him to arrive, so he decided to go to him. He asked the neighbors for help, after introducing himself to them in impressive English as the son of Mansour, the Syrian from Mount Lebanon who lived there. He told them he'd been studying medicine in Beirut and had come there to complete his studies before returning home. Even more impressed than before, they welcomed him and promised to look after his things. He wanted to tell them he subscribed to Darwin's theory and to ask them what they thought of it. But he paused, remembering the Frenchman who sold him a ticket. He also wanted to tell them that he'd come there to learn the culture of the great

American people and to bring parts of it, as appropriate, back home later. But he told himself the time would come.

Fares carried himself like a civilized foreign visitor and bought a map of the city and the streetcar lines. He made note of the stations where the streetcar would stop on the way to the port where those who passed the medical exam disembarked (though, to be fair, those who didn't pass were few and far between).

Fares, son of Mansour, son of Hashem, was the very first Syrian to buy a map in an unfamiliar city and use it to find his way!

He traveled first class, unlike the vast majority of New Yorkers. He was virtually the only olive-skinned individual in the cabin, where there was not a single Black person to be found. He felt he was darker than when he was in Beirut! Some people looked at him with blatant contempt. Others glanced at him out of the corner of their eyes and ignored him: People like him did not travel first class. Still others treated him no differently than any other passenger. But Fares held his head high with pride, looking around to make sure that what he knew of New York by way of his missionary professors or what he'd read, heard, and seen photographed was true. If one of them had asked him why he rode first class, he'd have proclaimed, loudly enough for all to hear, that he'd finished his second year of medical school, that he'd come to America to complete his studies, that he would return to his homeland afterward. But Fares wouldn't have told them he was also coming to take in as much as possible about the culture of the great American nation to bring back home. He didn't want to appear lesser in their eyes, if he could avoid it.

Lots of people had gathered in areas near the steamships' mooring by the time Fares reached the port. Soon his gaze fell upon his father, and he rushed toward him. Fares called out to him in Arabic, as if he were in Beirut:

"*Béyye*! *Béyye*!"

He continued pushing forward and calling out until he got close to him and his father heard him. He was confused to see his son coming from the opposite direction.

Mansour had his gaze fixed on the arrivals. He inspected them carefully, one by one, for fear that he wouldn't spot Fares before he'd already passed on to the medical examination center. Fares had grown older over many long years of absence, and his appearance had surely changed.

Rashid passed through without recognizing Mansour, even though Fares had given him his father's description and asked him to tell Mansour to wait for Fares at home if possible. But Rashid was distracted by his relatives, who'd all flocked around to spot him walking by and confirm that he'd arrived safely. Besides, trying to talk to the others who were waiting was no small feat.

When his father asked where his things were, Fares answered that they were at the neighbors' place! He told Mansour how he'd crossed the ocean in first class, how proud he was to have been treated with such deference. His father tried to alert him to the streets they crossed and the towering buildings they walked by. But each time Fares already knew what street it was and what the building was called, and each time his father grew more astonished.

It was really like Fares was remembering, not discovering. He knew the streets, he knew the buildings. Not only did he know the name of St. John's Burying Ground at the end of Broadway, he even knew the names of some of the burials and where their graves were located!

"I remember!" he'd answer his father, who appeared increasingly amazed each time and asked Fares how he knew that. But Mansour hadn't taken notice of what his son had said.

It wasn't a new world to Fares—not because he'd passed through Marseille and Paris, but because he *knew* this city. It was like he was coming back, not visiting for the first time.

It's true that hearing about something is not the same as seeing it. But Fares wasn't stupefied like the other Syrian migrants from Mount Lebanon. It didn't surprise him that there was nothing Ottoman or Turkish in sight. He wasn't startled by the electric lights, the trains and streetcars, the paved roads and enormous buildings, the clothing and smells—especially the smells!—the storefronts, the men, the women, unveiled and unaccompanied, and so on. None of that surprised him because he'd already heard and read about it, and because he'd seen some of it in Marseille, then in Paris—a global metropolis! Yet this was an experience he'd never had before.

But it was his reason for coming to America that distracted him from everything else. It hadn't left his mind for a moment, nor would it. As such, the first earnest conversation he had with his father was on this subject. Fares told him about everything that was going on: He inquired about the cost of studying medicine, and the money he had was entirely insufficient. He might be able to save enough over a year or two to cover the expenses.

Fares quickly realized that he couldn't entirely rely on his father, and that he would need to work before he'd be able to enter university to complete his specialization. He made the decision at that moment without any resentment or ill will toward his father. He didn't regret traveling first class and declining to stay in cheap hostels. He didn't see it as a waste—it was his right; it brought dignity to him and his country.

At the same time, Mansour advised him to take a few days to recover from the exhaustion of travel before starting work. But Fares wasn't as tired as the rest of the migrants in the lower classes. He had no time to waste: The future, and the homeland, were waiting for him. So he bought newspapers the day after he arrived and started reading the job offerings, marking down suitable possibilities. He'd leave on time after locating the addresses on the map, but it was no use: Each time, he arrived too late.

"A Syrian, are you? We just hired someone who came in earlier."

Over a week went by like this, and Fares hadn't found a job.

Then someone suggested that he go directly to the businesses, most of which were shops, and ask the owners if they needed a worker. But he was unsuccessful there, too. He felt like a failure, like the horizons were narrowing. Once, he even started to feel like there wasn't enough air and that he couldn't breathe. That scared him. He began to think he was a true stranger in a country he adored and had always dreamt of. He began to lose hope that there was a suitable place for him under this country's sky, even temporarily, just so he could finish his studies and return home.

But Mansour, who had gotten to know the country, constantly reassured him that he'd find work and, in the worst-case scenario, Fares could work with him as a peddler.

"You carry a box that you fill up with wares. You'd walk with me at first, then split off and do things your way on your own. I'll train you first—I'll show you the roads and teach you how to talk to people, especially women, so they're not afraid of you. I'll teach you where to sleep and that you shouldn't stay out too late, in case you wind up somewhere deserted when night falls or get caught off guard by rain or snow."

One of his relatives visited around this time and proposed that Fares accompany his sister Jamileh. She was about forty years old and had worked as a peddler for twenty-five years—five of which she'd spent unmarried and the other twenty as a widow. Her fiancé, one of her cousins, came to join her after five years of hesitation: He was afraid of the sea. He promised to join her as soon as possible before she made the journey, but he kept postponing out of intense fear. Upon her insistence and threatening to leave him, he finally decided to come to her. But the poor soul passed away aboard the steamship somewhere in the Atlantic just one week before reaching New York. His body was thrown overboard and, as Jamileh used to lament whenever she spoke of him, "the fish ate him!"

From that day forward, Jamileh refused to eat fish.

Her fiancé was a strong, handsome young man—"like the moon! He spoke well and smelled nice. He was friendly and always had a smile on his face. He was dependable, courageous, and resolute, and his mouth smelled of musk!"

Fares felt lost as the widowed Jamileh told him that. He couldn't figure out what she meant or why she was telling him. Each time she said it, Fares used to put his palm over his mouth and breathe into it to check how his breath smelled.

Distraught over the death of her fiancé, Jamileh took a vow of chastity and decided she'd never marry. And, although she never did, she introduced herself as a widow.

So Fares accompanied her at his cousin's suggestion and his father's encouragement. She was glad to fulfill her brother's request.

And thus Fares began his journey as a traveling salesman.

# 19

For the first several days, he watched what Jamileh did as he accompanied her door to door. After a few days of observation, Fares asked his father to give him a box called a *káshshe* filled with wares. His father obliged, so Fares set off on a sales trip with Jamileh to New Jersey, close to New York. Everyone was surprised that he managed to sell more than Jamileh herself—beautiful, experienced Jamileh who inspired confidence.

A few days later, Fares asked his father for a small *káshshe* filled with items that were lightweight yet valuable—silk scarves and tablecloths, expensive necklaces and bracelets—instead of cheap, bulky things, which he placed in a large box. At the threshold of the first door he knocked on, Fares sold the lady of the house a silk shawl, a necklace, and a bracelet. She paid him the price he asked for without haggling, and on top of that she gave him a tip. He was ashamed of himself for having raised the price of what he'd sold her on the assumption that she would negotiate, the way people do in our country.

"They're good people," he thought to himself.

He and Jamileh used to agree to meet at a specific location before sunset, then head back together to the place where they'd sleep. Sometimes she ran late, which worried him. Once, he waited for her under a tree near an unoccupied wooden cabin. By the time she finally returned, night had fallen and the contours of the road had vanished from sight.

"You're always late," he scolded her, then added reproachfully, "and we've been in the same neighborhoods!"

The weather got cold and it suddenly began to rain, so they pried off the cabin door and took shelter inside. She asked him to hold on to her to keep each other warm. When he hesitated, she went ahead and wrapped herself around him tightly so as not to leave any gap between their bodies for cold air to pass through. After they'd spent an hour trying to overcome the cold, the temperature unexpectedly dropped further, and they realized that the time for rest had passed them by that night. Fares worried that he was going to die at that instant, in a foreign country, without having achieved any of his dreams. He cried without drawing the attention of his cousin, who could sense his anxiety and fear. She instructed him to take out anything made of cloth from their boxes to bundle themselves in—life is more precious than anything else. She stepped out of the cabin for a moment, then came back in a bit wet, carrying a bundle of twigs. She opened a bottle of perfume and poured some of it onto a silk tablecloth, which she set alight beneath the sticks.

The sticks were damp and didn't catch fire easily. After great effort and patience, up came a flame that lit up the cabin. It became clear that they were in a graveyard, between two old, dilapidated coffins. Two skeletons became visible. Jamileh shrieked, and in the blink of an eye she darted out of the cabin and into the rain. Fares kept his calm, recalling the theft of bodies from the graveyards. He stepped outside to convince her to come back in lest she die of exposure. She agreed and reentered, though with her hands covering her eyes. She lowered her hands as Fares blindfolded her with a silk towel so she wouldn't accidentally open them and have to see the coffins and what was inside them. Then he pulled her close to keep out the air, and they lay down next to the fire, drifting in and out of wakefulness. They continued to cling to each other, though not only because of the cold. As dawn approached, it continued to rain a mixture of ice and water. Worried that the sleet would turn into a true snowfall and block their way, they decided to set out toward the nearest inhabited place.

As the morning progressed and things became visible, Fares was ashamed to look directly at his cousin. He wondered whether what had happened between them was as normal to her as it seemed.

Fares later began working by himself. He delighted housewives with his urbane English, which piqued their curiosity and prompted them to ask him questions. It was an opportunity for him to talk about Beirut, about its various schools that taught European languages. He didn't hesitate to tell them that he'd completed his second year of medical school and that he was working to save up enough to continue his studies. They usually enjoyed listening to these stories, asked him more questions, and invited him in to have something to eat and drink. Sometimes they tried to make use of his medical knowledge and asked him about discomfort they were experiencing—though some of them were faking it. He was reluctant to make advances at first but later grew comfortable with it. One time, he had to flee through the window when the husband unexpectedly returned.

Fares was proud of his dalliances with housewives. It made him feel like America was not unobtainable, but within reach.

He roamed through all the towns and urban peripheries surrounding New York City, spending the nights at cheap inns.

He spent one night in Montclair, New Jersey, in an attic above a shop owned by a Lebanese. With him were several other Lebanese peddlers, which wouldn't have been unusual or even notable . . . if not for the fact that the police raided the place that night. They arrested two merchants sleeping next to him who were accused of theft, and he feared for his own safety. His dismay was twofold because the thieves were his countrymen. Besides, stealing is wrong in itself and contradicts the morals of any nation.

The truth was, Fares was generally displeased with the behavior of his countrymen in the United States, especially in so-called Little Syria. This was an area located along Washington Street and some of the surrounding side roads, where the most significant community of immigrants from Ottoman Syria, especially Mount Lebanon, was located. Thus, he resolved to keep his distance from them to get away from their problems and the virus of unpunctuality they carried with them from their country. The New York police often had to intervene to resolve their issues. One day, they came to blows with clubs and knives; people were injured and transported to the hospital. The greatest battle was between the Greek Orthodox and the Maronites. At the time, there were very few Druze, Sunni, or Shi'i immigrants. Syrian Muslims weren't a large enough minority community to assert their presence, or to cause problems.

*The New York Times* reported on a brawl that took place on Washington Street in which his relatives were involved. Although several were wounded, they weren't taken to the hospital, for fear that they'd be arrested and prosecuted. One of them badly needed medical attention, and none other than Fares was forced to treat him. Had the police found out, they'd have thrown him in jail, then deported him, but Fares had no choice. He repeatedly considered telling the police, but he was afraid: His people could only interpret something like that as treachery.

Fares quickly decided to distance himself from Washington Street. A few days after the incident, he began living by himself on Grant Street, two buildings away from Broadway, in a small second-floor room above a cobbler's shop. From that area, it was very easy to get anywhere in New York and to the neighboring cities and towns.

Around that time, Fares ran into Hasna, the girl from Brasha whom he was briefly in a relationship with. Her father had been involved in the brawl and got grazed by a knife that nearly got the better of him. He went into hiding for a few weeks until the wound had completely healed. Fares visited him at the insistence of Mansour, who accompanied him. There he met Hasna, as he'd expected—in fact, just as his father had surely intended. Mansour had learned of their previous relationship from his siblings in Mount Lebanon and from other sources.

Fares was very pleased to encounter Hasna, whom he found beautiful, mature, and alluring. They made plans to meet, and did so several times, unbeknownst to their families. But eventually she insisted that he ask her father's permission to marry her so they'd be officially engaged, at which point she'd wait as long as he liked. And so it was—they decided to marry as soon as Fares finished medical school. They got engaged in the presence of his father, her parents, and their relatives and friends.

Fares's engagement was an additional incentive to work and save money, which he already did as much as possible. He only spent money on the necessities, except when he'd visit a prostitute on occasion. That, to him, was a necessity. Prostitutes were a gateway into each country his work led him to. They offered familiarity amid the isolation of being far from home. Things didn't change much after the engagement: His fiancée remained in New York, so he only saw her once a week when he came back, sometimes more. Hasna was a virgin, and she didn't let him (nor did he let himself) take any further liberties with her body before marriage. Besides, Fares had taken a liking to prostitutes ever since first becoming aware of the sensual world. He saw no harm in mingling with them.

At that stage, he sought out the company of prostitutes who were lower in price. These were older Americans and Europeans, somewhat younger Italians and Greeks, and young women from China and elsewhere in Asia.

# 20

Then Fares came across another way to earn and save money that complemented his main work, peddling. The recommendation letters written by his professors and other missionaries were of paramount importance in this unexpected regard.

Every so often, these letters helped him find work that allowed him to make some money giving lectures on Palestine—the land where the Lord Jesus was born. Many Americans at the time were eager to learn about the area and enjoyed hearing stories about it. Fares was successful in getting summoned from time to time to give a lecture on the place he came from. He told audiences about how people lived, where they lived, what they ate and drank, their customs around marriage, birth, and death. They really enjoyed when he described his relatives' houses in the village from which his father had migrated. Their homes composed of a single room with stone walls and had roofs made of dirt about twenty to thirty centimeters thick, which rested on wooden planks covered with sharp thistle thorns. The room was rectangular, most of it used as living space for sleeping, eating, sitting, and receiving guests. The other area, which was smaller and lower into the ground, was for animals.

"Jesus was born in a place like this!" Fares would remark.

He'd describe the mountains, the valleys and plains, the Mediterranean coast, the snowy peaks of Mount Lebanon. He told them about the centuries-old cedars that were used to build Solomon's temple, the palaces of emperors and kings, and the fleets with which the Phoenicians, the Greeks, the Romans, and the Arabs conquered the world.

Fares described the region as it is reported in the Old Testament, with which they were quite familiar. He used the Scripture as a starting point to go into detail, and as a way to make things easier for them to understand. In so doing Fares hoped to engender in them a love of our country. To them, it was the Land of Prophethood—an impression he reinforced in their minds.

Fares wasn't a practicing believer like many people were at that time. But he used to read passages from the Bible before going to lecture.

Not for a moment did Fares forget that he had to earn money to continue his studies. There was only one thing that used to make his eyes well up: when he passed by a university and saw students carrying books under their arms, gathering together, coming and going.

One day, Fares was carrying his *kâshshe* near Yale University in New Haven, Connecticut, on his way to a small village. One of the Syrian peddlers had told him about a woman there who wanted to buy her daughter a gold necklace and herself a silk scarf. He stood and watched the students, recalling the two years he'd spent at the American University of Beirut. All of a sudden, a man approached and asked Fares to produce a work permit. The request perplexed Fares, but soon he realized that the man was a police officer and that he was being serious.

Fares answered that he'd never been told that a peddler needed a permit.

"Didn't they teach you that in your country?" the officer replied.

Fares may have loved America, but he did not appreciate his country being slandered. He didn't like the way the policeman was talking to him.

Fares loved America. He knew its history, geography, economy, and culture better than the officer did. Fares knew America's value and importance in the world better than the officer did. But he didn't like this kind of language, these comparisons between the Ottoman Empire and America—the America of freedom, of living in dignity, of respect for the human person, of law and institutions.

America, where women were free to work, to choose their husbands. Fares even felt that women had a little too much freedom in certain circles in America. They were free to remain unmarried, to live alone wherever they wished—even to live *with* whomever they wished, at times out of wedlock.

None of that existed in Ottoman Syria, as Fares knew very well. So he didn't appreciate people talking to him like that.

"Didn't anyone over there teach you that everyone's supposed to know the law?" the officer continued. "And that ignorance of the law doesn't excuse breaking it?"

Fares wasn't sure what to say. His bewilderment came to a head when the officer grabbed him and marched him forward, before he found himself in jail.

Despite having promised himself to acquit himself like a model citizen while living in America, despite coming there to bring back the parts of its culture that befit his country, Fares was now behind bars. He had no idea who to ask for help, who'd be able to help him, or how to reach such a person.

*Which way will you turn, Fares?*

Like someone wandering in the desert alone!

It had been before noon that Fares was jailed, and by now it was evening. The more time went by, the sadder he became. But he took solace in the fact that he'd get to sleep free of charge somewhere no worse than the places where he usually slept while peddling.

Fares wasn't like most Syrians, who spent their free time reminiscing about life in their homeland, in their villages, on their mountains, near freshwater springs in the valleys and foothills. They recalled past exploits back home as they smoked *argileh* on Washington Street, drank *arak*, and sang *'atéba*s and *mijéna*s as their eyes welled up and they shook their heads ruefully.[1] Fares was a pragmatist. He lived not in the past but in the present, for the sake of the future. He wasn't like the others who used to say that the East was the spirit and the West the body, the East was emotion and the West the intellect. Fares believed the West was the future of the East and that if the East didn't westernize, it would languish in the abyss of history, shuffling along at the tail end of humanity.

1. The *'atéba* is a Levantine musical form, often improvised and mournful in tone, with lyrics associated with rural life, exile, and longing. A *mijéna* is a refrain often added to an *'atéba* song.

So Fares didn't cry or allow himself to be discouraged over the distress he'd experienced. Instead, he thought about what he'd have to do to get out of this jail quickly, lest this black spot mar the tale of his stay in America. But what was he to do?

Fares was always cautious. He carried the recommendation letters, his prized possessions, in a small bag that he wore beneath his clothes. In the morning, when an officer brought him his breakfast—a piece of bread, a small portion of cold corn, and a cup of tea—Fares tried to carry on a conversation with him for as long as possible so he could properly introduce himself.

The officer who brought Fares breakfast was not the same one who'd thrown him in jail. This officer was totally different from his counterpart from the previous night: more humane and educated. He was genuinely impressed by Fares's command of English, which Fares made an effort to put on display to prove he was different from the other migrants, who couldn't speak, read, or write English—who were illiterate even in their own language. The policeman took interest in Fares's story and expressed willingness to help him. He agreed to deliver one of the letters Fares had brought from Beirut to a Protestant clergyman who oversaw the New Haven region.

The pastor, despite being very ill and bedridden, took interest in Fares's predicament and sent for his lawyer, whom he asked to go get Fares out of jail.

Fares was very fortunate that the pastor invited him to spend the night. Moreover, the man was a reader of *The Missionary Herald*, a magazine that chronicled the activities of American Protestant missionaries all over the world. Beirut was one of their most important outposts in Asia, so the pastor knew some things about the Syrian Protestant College (today the American University of Beirut). He'd heard about the fate of Asaad al-Shidyaq, Syria's first Protestant martyr, according to the missionaries. The first thing he asked Fares to do after helping him get out of jail was to tell him about Shidyaq in detail. The pastor had little affection or respect for the Christians of the East and had been influenced by the views of the early missionaries and their correspondences in this magazine. He mentioned the name Isaac Bird, for one, and asked what Fares thought of him. The pastor also knew about the massacres the Christians of Mount Lebanon suffered in 1860. But he was of the opinion that they'd been the aggressors, and that divine providence had punished them by means of Druze fanatics in the mountains and the ignorant masses in Damascus—clearing the way for Protestantism to proliferate further.

This lively conversation, punctuated by involuntary pauses and coughing, at the pastor's bedside made Fares uneasy. In the East, you didn't argue with someone about their religion. One would sooner kill another person belonging to a different religion or sect than take issue with their beliefs. Fares tried to change the subject at every opportunity, until all of a sudden the pastor asked him about his own faith. Fares gave an answer that made him realize things weren't quite so simple.

"My religion is the welfare of people of every creed!" he proclaimed. "My religion is the advancement of my country that languishes under the yoke of ignorance, injustice, and subjugation. My religion is the good of all humanity!"

The pastor said nothing.

The pastor's sixteen-year-old daughter, Jessie, was there and listened to what Fares was saying with striking attentiveness. Her presence motivated him to speak well, in eloquent English, which he'd improved significantly during his stay in America through practice as well as reading. He assiduously set aside long hours on his days off to review medical textbooks in preparation to reenter university, and to read literature. This he did at public libraries, which he was astonished to find everywhere he went.

In the morning, all of them except the father had breakfast together: the pastor's wife, his daughter Jessie, and his younger son. As the mother explained, their older, married daughter was at home with her husband and children, and their eldest son was an army officer at West Point.

Fares was caught off guard by this reception and hospitality. He realized that some Americans are even more hospitable than Syrians, albeit in their own way.

Over breakfast, Jessie grew more interested in this intelligent, olive-skinned young man, who hailed from the land where Christ was born and had walked upon its soil. Her eyes would light up when her gaze fell directly upon him. As he bade her and her mother farewell at the doorstep, she asked him to bring her a silk tablecloth for her desk, no matter the cost, as well as a carving of a cedar tree into a plank made of wood from the cedars of Lebanon, which appear several times in the Old Testament and ancient Eastern mythology. She asked him when he'd be back next, and he promised to return as soon as possible. No one but Fares took notice of how she listened as he told them about his country. When he looked at her, he felt that the roots of his tree ran deep within America. It worried him that he began to feel as though those eyes, that hair and complexion, that figure, that gaze, could possibly lead him to put down roots in America and settle there permanently. His country sprang to mind and punished him for his digression. How could a person forget his country? Betray it?

As he departed from the distant village he'd initially sought out prior to his arrest, Fares wanted to stop by to see the family again. But he was reluctant: He didn't want his secret, though still a mere seed scarcely visible to the naked eye, to come to light—the secret of the pastor's young daughter. But when he reached the spot where the policeman had stopped him, Fares headed toward the university instead of proceeding to the train station. He asked for directions to the office of the dean, whom he asked for permission to meet with briefly, albeit unannounced. The dean didn't object and listened intently as Fares told him his life story. He read the recommendation letters from Fares's professors and the missionaries and commended him for his resolve. But he advised Fares to choose another university, because this one—Yale—was wildly expensive and would be difficult for him to afford. The dean was so impressed with Fares that he wrote him a recommendation letter to present to whichever university he decided to enroll in.

# 21

Fares returned to his studies after working for three years and saving as much as he could. He was somewhat able to rely on his father, whose circumstances had improved over the years. Mansour had opened a shop in New Jersey and started supplying Lebanese immigrants with merchandise rather than wandering from town to town himself. He'd also begun renting out the attic above the shop to *káshshe* salesmen from his country. It had room for five customers, sometimes more, which tangibly increased his income.

Before returning to school, Fares had broken off his engagement with Hasna. This was a big problem, first for himself but especially between him and his father.

Fares had given serious thought to ending his relationship from the moment his eyes met Jessie's in New Haven. He regretted having gotten engaged and resolved to await the opportunity to extricate himself from the agreement. And so he did. When he'd decided to resume his studies, he met with Hasna in his room on Grand Street in New York City. He apologized that he was unable to keep his promise. He told her this decision was for her benefit more than his own, so she could sort out her affairs from that moment on: He didn't know what fate had in store for him. For her part, Hasna tried to convince him that she'd wait as long as he liked, so long as he kept his promise, but he refused. It was no easy task for him to say no as she stood before him in all her beauty, with her figure and complexion, effusing the scent of the homeland.

Mansour was angry when he learned what happened.

"It's unlike us, as Syrians, for a young man to promise to marry a girl, in public—in the presence of his father and her parents—then to break his word," he explained. "It's true we're in America, taking in American culture. But we still come from Mount Lebanon. The morals of our country that we carry in our souls will endure so long as we live!

"This is an engagement, a promise to be kept! *Waláw*—what, have you forgotten about your country?!"

Fares's father wanted him to marry a Lebanese girl to keep America from swallowing him up.

"Son, we're here temporarily," Mansour reminded him, "no matter how long we end up staying."

But Fares stood his ground, even as something deep within him implored him to make good on his promise. Whenever he felt that urge, which seemed to emanate all the way from home, he remembered Jessie's eyes—Jessie, who was still waiting for him to bring her the items she'd ordered from him. He remembered her pure skin, her tall build, her innocent gaze, her enthrallment with him. He was convinced that through Jessie, America would open up its gates before him and reveal its treasures, that he'd grow wings and be able to fly.

Hasna's father broke off contact with Fares, then passed a message along to Mansour through an intermediary.

*Nothing is more precious than dignity. We're still Easterners, whether or not we live in America. Even if your son changes his mind, our daughter is off the table!*

Abu Fares empathized with the girl's father. But that didn't stop him from sticking up for his son, so that Fares could realize their shared dream of becoming a doctor.

Three years of working as a peddler enabled Fares to save seven thousand dollars. It was enough money to complete his training without having to turn to his father or go back to work. But that young American woman was waiting for him to bring her a silk scarf and a cedar carving.

Mansour, aware of his son's financial situation, was surprised when Fares asked him for a small *káshshe* so he could go make a sale. Even more astonishing was that he asked for a silk scarf and a plank of cedarwood with a Lebanese cedar carved into it. Mansour was suspicious, though he didn't let on. But now his eyes were open, so he proceeded with caution when it came to his son's life . . . lest he encounter a surprise that wouldn't be easy to accept. Abu Fares couldn't handle the idea of his son marrying an American woman who was a stranger to our country, our morals, our customs.

Fares wrote to Jessie several times to assure her that he'd bring her what she ordered, and she'd write back concisely to thank him. One time she asked him for his university address all of a sudden. It didn't make sense: How could he be a university student and a peddler at the same time? He eventually wrote back to say he'd be with her at the end of November—on Thanksgiving, one of the biggest holidays in America. He'd chosen that date because he had ten days off from classes.

He wouldn't accept payment for the things he sold her—he gave them to her for free. Dumbfounded, she dashed over to her mother with joy, telling her that Fares the Syrian wouldn't accept payment for her items. Jessie presented her mother with the gifts and danced around like a cheerful songbird. Her mother approached Fares and thanked him, but she didn't invite him to lunch. Fares had been certain she'd do so, given her hospitality the previous time and the friendliness of her husband, the pastor. His health had declined, so Fares was unfortunately unable to see him.

"Thank you, Jessie!" he said, having worked up the courage to address her by name as she accompanied him to the gate of the yard leading to the street to say goodbye.

Fares had hoped to tell her, at the table with her mother, about the developments that he'd been through since the first time he met them. But things didn't go the way he expected. On his way out, he managed to quickly tell her that he'd resumed his studies at university, as conveyed in the letters he'd written. He couldn't say more—her mother stood at the window, bidding him farewell with a wave of her hand, awaiting her daughter's return.

"Write to me all the time!" she whispered to him.

"I'll spend tonight at the Belleview Hotel, in New Haven. The train leaves tomorrow at noon," he said, whispering back so her mother wouldn't hear. Then he raised his hand in farewell as he turned and headed back.

Fares didn't leave the hotel at all that day, worried that Jessie might show up and not be able to find him. Normally, when he had free time, he would go out and explore the tourist attractions, wander the city, visit museums, browse libraries to apprise himself of recent publications, and read newspapers in cafés . . . just like any American medical student enrolled at a respected university would do.

He would also write to his friends who were back home and to his fellow migrants, telling them what he was up to and about the things he'd seen, asking in turn about their lives and about the country. He corresponded especially with Jurji in Cairo. He had, of course, learned that Jurji had not been admitted to the Qasr El Eyni medical school and ultimately shifted focus toward literature and journalism: He planned to write books, found a publishing house called Dar al-Hilal (Crescent House), and publish a magazine to spread knowledge across the Arab world and motivate Arabs to get back on their feet after having stumbled for far too long. In their letters, Fares and Jurji exchanged views and revealed secrets about how they ought to work with others for the sake of the Nahda. They spoke of the secret societies they were thinking of establishing, the kind that would certainly be dangerous, for them and for others, to discuss publicly. Time and again they made plans to meet in Beirut, but circumstances prevented them from doing so.

As he sat in the hotel café that day, Fares wrote to his good friend Saadeddine al-Jabawi, who'd risen through the ranks of the police force, gotten married, and had children. He still shared the ambitions of the educated elite to achieve the dream of a modern state.

Fares's prediction proved accurate: Jessie showed up, and, thankfully, he hadn't left the hotel. He might've lost his mind if he hadn't been there when she arrived. He got anxious when he saw her and worried he might faint. He wasn't prepared for this onslaught of unfamiliar emotions. He wasn't ready for America, with all her splendor and her bright horizon, to approach him, shake his hand, and sit with him over a glass of orange juice.

He told her that he was very happy to be studying medicine again. In two years, he'd be a doctor. What he didn't mention was that he was going to return to his country after that. It saddened him to keep this from her, not because it was a lie—and it wasn't!—but because he feared telling her would get in the way of what was starting to take shape between them.

*The homeland! Don't forget yours!*

*Forget your name, but don't forget where you come from, Fares!*

*Forget the color of your eyes, but don't forget the lofty mountains enveloped in clouds and crowned in snow.*

*Don't forget the flourishing plains irrigated with pure water and the sweat of brows. Don't forget the vast sky that holds the pureness of dawn, the four seasons, the distant blue sea, the gushing springs, the brooks and rivers.*

*Don't forget your countrymen weighed down by ignorance, poverty, and disease. Don't forget your homeland beset by misery and far afield of the civilized world.*

This is what went through Fares's mind, what he said to himself at that time. But going back wasn't an option right now. The issue at hand was Jessie.

Fares bid her farewell, deciding to conceal his feelings for her until the right moment came along to reveal them—in the hope that she, too, was waiting for the right day to do the same. What nourished his dream was that she asked him to bring her hairpins, as if she'd forgotten he was no longer a peddler but once again a student who didn't have time for this.

And so he began to look forward to university holidays so he could visit her, under the pretext of selling her the small items she'd requested. Then he'd meet her at the hotel café. His love for her quickly deepened, and he eagerly awaited the moment when he could reveal his affections. Jessie, too, was concealing her feelings. She spent their time together asking him questions about his studies, about the distant lands where Jesus Christ was born, about its climate, its waters, its flora and fauna, about the people there and their way of life—did they still maintain the same customs that were followed in Christ's day?

He'd take pleasure in telling her about his country until the time came for her to return home. Then she'd ask him to bring her some other items, giving him an excuse to come back.

How could she *not* have been concealing something?

# 22

One day Jessie's mother stumbled upon a letter that Fares had written to her daughter. There was nothing particularly suspicious about it: brief updates about his university studies and when he planned to visit next. But, in and of itself, the letter aroused suspicion: Why would this Syrian peddler be writing to her daughter as if he were her friend?

And then he gave her his university address!

What could explain this furtiveness?

How had things gotten so mixed up?

The mother informed her husband about the letter, despite his deteriorating health. The news then reached Jessie's older brother, an American army officer, who became deeply concerned by the matter. He approached his father and asked him to dissuade her from continuing her communication with Fares.

"It makes no sense for the sister of a US Army officer to form a connection with a Syrian—some Turk from Mount Lebanon—whose skin is dark, whose background and family I know nothing about, who works as a peddler, yet whose address is a university! Even if their relationship is innocent and purely platonic, it could turn into something we'd be better off without."

Jessie's brother feared she'd end up marrying this "Turk," who could very well be after her family's reputation (in the city and across the state) and her share of the inheritance, worth about twenty-five thousand dollars.

He was also worried about his own future. He sought to make his way to a high rank in the army; failing that, he planned to enter politics and run for local office, relying on his good reputation in the military and the credibility of their father, the pastor.

When Jessie's father learned that Fares was indeed studying medicine at the university, he began to doubt the young man's intentions: Why would he still be working as a salesman? He wasted no time in asking his daughter why this young man had visited her several times. Feigning innocence, she replied that he only worked in peddling on his days off so he could afford tuition.

The family agreed that Jessie must ask this man to stop seeing her, and that she had to stop buying things from him. The consensus was so absolute that she couldn't find even the slightest crack to voice a criticism. She grudgingly kept quiet, then agreed to respect their wishes.

When Fares came by at the usual time on his day off from class, she was the only one to receive him. She didn't buy the items that she'd requested, claiming that he hadn't brought what she'd asked for. She managed to whisper that she would explain everything to him the next day at the hotel.

Fares was incredulous. The wide world had suddenly collapsed on him. America had slammed its doors in his face. He'd lost the world, and lost himself. In that moment, he wished that he'd stayed in Lebanon, that he hadn't let his sense of dignity shape his actions toward the administration at the American University of Beirut. He wished he hadn't participated in the strikes during the Darwin affair, that he had stayed in Egypt with his friends Jurji Zaidan and Amin Fleihan.

She told him that her entire family was uncomfortable with their relationship—that they'd told her to stop buying his trinkets and to forbid him from visiting.

"What about you?" Fares asked, nearly losing consciousness.

"Me?" she replied, then added with a sigh, "I'm willing to do whatever you suggest."

Fares, unable to believe what he was hearing, took a deep breath and said, "In the East, we have a proverb that says, 'Every young woman is a guest in her parents' home.'"

"What do you mean?" Jessie asked.

He was confused about how to reply. But he was already in too deep to back down and needed to find a way out. It was the first time he'd spoken to her so candidly and directly. Their past conversations had consisted of cryptic hints, of emotions couched in business transactions. But time had them cornered now. They needed to make a decision, and he needed to take the initiative.

"What do you mean?" she repeated, eager for his response. It was like she was waiting for the magical solution that only those with brown skin who came from the faraway Orient—the land of wisdom and spirituality—knew how to find.

He explained that a young woman's true home was at her husband's house. He told her about the happiness marriage provides, about its inescapable necessity.

She didn't reply.

The meeting ended with them agreeing that from that day onward they'd meet at the hotel, without his coming to the house.

They decided Fares would address a letter to the family's Polish housemaid, who couldn't read English. That way, Jessie's parents would assume it was written in Polish and not bat an eye. Jessie told the housemaid about the plan and asked her to give her the letter, which bore a special mark, as soon as it arrived. She urged her not to tell anyone the secret. The maid had a special love for Jessie because of how kind and generous Jessie was to her.

From that point on, Fares threw himself even more deeply into his studies, decreased his leisure time, and even decided to visit prostitutes only in the most desperate of times—despite how difficult it was for him to adhere to this plan. He wanted to be deserving of Jessie's love, her sacrifice and pure intentions.

But the maid told her parents the secret once they noticed she'd been receiving an unusual amount of letters. They decided as a result to pressure her daughter into marrying an American from the Lenn family. The Lenns were well respected in the city and owned land, shops, and shares in the railroad company. They were particularly known for their philanthropic work and helping build public libraries.

How could Fares Mansour Hashem—the Lebanese-Syrian-Turkish immigrant of average height, with dark hair, olive skin, and black eyes—compete with a tall, blond-haired, blue-eyed American Protestant from a wealthy family who'd earned an engineering degree less than a year ago?

Jessie's sister, who was married, told her that Eastern men marry dozens of women—did she want to be one of them? Her brother, the officer, told her that if she married Fares, he'd resign from the army and abandon his political ambitions.

To be even more careful, the siblings decided to enlist the services of a detective agency to monitor Fares's movements. Despite the two having agreed to meet less often, the private investigators spotted them together in the courtyard of the Belleview Hotel one day. They noticed she followed him up to his room and stayed there for about an hour! She'd come to tell him they needed to accept reality. And she did indeed come up to his room, where they were alone. They embraced for a long time, and she allowed him to kiss her on the neck and the cheek. She also kissed him on the cheek.

"Goodbye!" she said, and left.

Jessie had no choice but to submit to her parents' wishes, and Fares had no choice but to accept his destiny in America.

But the surprise came when the police arrived at the hotel where he was staying and asked him to show them his peddling permit. Fares replied that he had stopped peddling—he was a medical student now. In response, they presented him with the shawl he had given Jessie less than an hour earlier.

By the time the sun began to set, he was on his way to jail.

# 23

Fares was convinced he'd fallen into a type of trap he never imagined he would fall into. He prepared to spend the night in his cell for the second time since his arrival in this distant land. Once again, he regretted coming. He wished that the strike hadn't happened. But the scent of Jessie that still filled his nose and lungs, his hearing and his dreams, made him forget his condition from time to time . . . until the cell door opened to let him out and his eyes fell on Jessie herself. She had come to tell the police that this shawl had been given to her as a gift from him.

When she'd realized that the shawl had disappeared, she went straight to her father to tell him what had happened. It took effort for him to draw the full story out of her. Once he understood—that a trap had been set for Fares—he longed to rise from his bed, but his body wouldn't allow it. Instead, he urged his daughter to hurry to the jail with a lawyer. She was to explain everything to him, who would then accompany her to the police station to make it clear to police: The shawl had been a gift, not something Fares had sold as a peddler.

Her father wished she'd end her relationship with Fares. He was uneasy about this man from a distant land. More than that, he feared the scorn and disapproval their marriage might provoke, both toward her and the family, in the heart of this traditional American community, in this deeply conservative city.

There was a story from that city that spread by word of mouth among Syrian immigrants. One of their countrymen bought a cow and put it in the field next to where he lived. His American neighbor became annoyed and sued him. Before the Syrian entered the courtroom, his lawyer advised him to hide the crucifix hanging from his neck, lest the judge see it and they lose the case! Bigotry against all things not white and Protestant was rampant in many circles there.

Nevertheless, the father didn't approve of the young man languishing in jail for unjust reasons.

Fares told the lawyer what really happened to him once they were alone. The lawyer reassured him that he'd do his best to have him released immediately. But he couldn't find Fares Mansour Hashem in the jail records—there was no date of his arrest. He was confused. He couldn't have Fares released on bail without knowing where the arrest warrant had been issued. He investigated the matter and discovered that a judge at a lower court just outside the city had issued the warrant. But it was already nine o'clock in the evening, and Fares would have to sleep in jail. He'd be released in the morning, his lawyer promised.

But, unfortunately for Fares, things got more complicated. Jessie's father, the pastor, died that evening. When the family noticed that he hadn't risen at his usual hour the next morning, they went to check on him and found his body lying still and cold in bed. As the doctor later confirmed, he had died at night, hours before they discovered him.

Shortly before his death, Jessie's father asked her if she truly wanted Fares.

"Yes," she answered without hesitation.

He nodded. "Give me some time," he said, "to make peace with your mother, your sister, and your brother."

But death denied him the chance to speak with his son, the officer, or with his married daughter—who was the most hostile of them all.

Her mother had obeyed her husband when he was alive. But now she refused to challenge her children, so she kept quiet. She told "her darling" Jessie that she wouldn't be able to sway her other children. Her mother's withdrawal from the affair didn't help Jessie at all.

As the crisis deepened, Jessie's mother withdrew into her room, rarely emerging. She made it clear that neither Jessie nor anyone else was to discuss the subject with her.

And so Fares remained in jail for months. Finally, Jessie signed an agreement with her siblings to relinquish her share of their father's inheritance. The siblings persuaded the lawyer not to seek Fares's release from jail until Jessie complied. They assumed he was after Jessie's share of their father's estate—a combination of cash, shares, and assets. It was a massive sum for a Syrian immigrant from the Ottoman East who, under the best of circumstances, might earn no more than ten or twenty dollars after a grueling day of work, enduring a long commute and dangerous conditions, as well as the vicissitudes of weather: heat and cold, rain and snow.

So Fares languished in prison for an entire month, as Jessie refused to be blackmailed. She was incredulous about what her siblings were doing to her.

The lawyer's conscience got the better of him, so he visited Fares in jail from time to time. Each time, he gave him ten dollars of his own money, claiming that he received the cash from a charity.

More importantly, the lawyer started delivering letters from Jessie by the second week. Fares was so thrilled to receive them that he'd forget he was unjustly behind bars. They made him feel free—like he was in the open air of Mount Lebanon, in the cedar, pine, and juniper forests, near the springs, surrounded by hills and plains stretching all the way to the sea. Jessie confessed her love to him and raised his morale, urging him to be patient.

Once Fares and Jessie had come to trust their lawyer, they told him they wished to marry once they'd put the ordeal behind them, which made him even more inclined to help them. At last, he revealed the truth: He had been unable to resist the pressure that was placed on him by Jessie's siblings, who refused to allow Fares's release until their sister forfeited her right to her father's inheritance.

Finally Jessie signed the contract—but only after watching her mother's health decline rapidly.

"Where the hell did this Syrian come from?!" her mother had asked. Jessie's decision was twofold. She decided to cede her inheritance rights to appease her family and, at the same time, to cut off her relationship with Fares and went back on her promise to marry him. It was as if she wanted to take revenge on herself—as if she were trying to absolve herself of guilt for her father's death and her mother's worsening health.

As he sat in the jail cell, Fares couldn't believe what she'd written. Suspecting that the lawyer was now in on some kind of conspiracy against him, he insisted on meeting Jessie in person so she could inform him of her decision face-to-face. Her siblings allowed her to meet him, on the condition that the lawyer be present. And so it was. To drive home the seriousness of her decision, Jessie told him that she was going to marry the man who planned to ask her hand.

"Think about the position I'm in!" she implored him, before bidding him farewell for good. "I've made my mother miserable, and probably accelerated my father's death, too."

By now, Fares had missed a lot of school—what would his excuse be? How would he catch up on all the material he'd missed? And, more importantly, how could he face the university administration if they found out that he'd been in jail? Would they expel him? Would all future universities reject him after that?

Had he lost his studies the same way he'd lost Jessie from America and Hasna from his village?

What about all his dreams to come back home as a doctor? His continued correspondence with Jurji, Saadeddine, and the others? And what about the oath he'd made with Jurji and Amin aboard the ship off the coast of Beirut?

His fears were confirmed when he returned to university and went to meet with the dean. The man told him the university was appalled to learn that one of its students had been jailed for taking advantage of an innocent young woman, and for violating American law by running a business without a special permit.

The words injured his personal and national dignity. After all, it was Fares who had been keen to give the best possible image of his country and its people. Worse still, the dean didn't give him any time to defend himself. He simply looked down to the papers in front of him, signaling that Fares needed to leave his office. The administration refused to give him a written confirmation of his enrollment and good standing.

Why were her siblings still waging a war they'd already won?

This was a moment of unbearable humiliation. And it was in this exact moment that Fares decided to enlist in the American army—to prove to anyone who doubted the goodness of his character, not only as an individual, but also as a Syrian, from the city of Beirut, which rivaled

Alexandria and Cairo in innovation and advancement, which was steadily transforming into something brilliant: the bride of all cities, the star of the Mediterranean. Joining the army, for him, was the greatest service a citizen could offer his homeland.

Everyone who knew of his relationship with Jessie would soon hear of Fares—in a different light.

Fares, the son of Beirut, was not about to let this insult go unanswered. Everyone responsible would come to regret it.

But Fares delayed enlisting in the army in order to take a break. It was a good thing he did, because when the lawyer learned of the university administration's decision through a letter from Fares, he requested to meet with the dean. During their meeting, he informed the dean of Fares's innocence, explaining that his imprisonment had been a mistake: The judge had gotten the name wrong when issuing the arrest warrant.

But the administration (under pressure, of course, from Jessie's siblings) was not entirely convinced by the lawyer's testimony. So they reversed the decision only partially. They issued Fares a certificate acknowledging his prior enrollment and his completed coursework. But they would not allow him to continue his studies there.

Fares, in spite of the news, didn't despair. He was able to enroll at another university with a good reputation—St. Louis University—without abandoning his decision to eventually enlist in the army, when the time was right: as soon as he completed his studies.

Fares spent his time before the start of the next semester selling goods, after obtaining a license this time. He hadn't come to this country to break its laws. He also spent time preparing for his studies, determined to raise his English to a level even higher than that of Americans themselves.

By taking on the values of true American citizenship, by enlisting in the army, he'd show everyone what Syrians are like—what Syrian soldiers are like: brave on the battlefield, devoted to serving the country and its higher principles.

"We aren't here just to take!" he would always tell the other Syrian migrants he met and those he corresponded with back home or elsewhere abroad. "We're here to give, too."

Fares excelled in all the courses that he took, even mathematics. He did well in anatomy, a subject that brought back memories of his university days in Beirut, of the bodies that had been stolen so students could learn the material. It also brought back memories of Yorma.

"Poor Yorma the martyr!" he said to himself. Yorma, the martyr of anatomy lessons at the American University of Beirut, victim of the campaign to stamp out superstitions, victim of his big mouth and the blabbing about what she'd been doing to him. But, in truth, he hadn't really revealed a secret; it was a tradition among the guys to swap stories about their encounters with prostitutes—the *sharamít,* as people had begun to call them in Beirut.

Then he recalled how he skipped anatomy class in Beirut when the cadaver belonged to his aunt.

*How distant those memories seem today!*

These feelings caught him off guard. "But this time the homeland is near," he reassured himself.

More than anything else, passing anatomy made him remember his mother. When it suddenly seemed to him that she belonged to another realm—another past life—he grew afraid.

"Zakiyya!" he exclaimed, calling her by name. "Imm Fares!" He said her name out loud to reassure her—and himself—that he was still himself, her boy Fares. That she was still his mother, who lived for him and for his siblings.

In his final semester before graduation, he asked his father for help so that he wouldn't have to work, as he usually did during school vacations.

He especially worked in the summers, saving what he could, since his university tuition was way more than expected. It wasn't just about tuition—it was also about room and board, food, textbooks, notebooks, pens, laboratory expenses, etcetera. On top of all that, the circles he was in required him to dress a certain way. There were leisure activities and cafés. Then there were prostitutes, whom he continued to visit from time to time—especially now that his relationship with Jessie had ended. This entertainment, he felt, was part of the job.

It was around this time that he met a Chinese prostitute who'd been in the country without legal papers since 1877. She'd fled California at the peak of the anti-Chinese riots that targeted immigrant laborers. He'd met her through a young Lebanese immigrant who used to sneak her into Fares's room at night.

Fares had a special relationship with prostitutes. He felt great empathy for them, rebelling inwardly against the harsh circumstances that had forced them into such a life. The plight of American prostitutes reminded him of the conditions back home: a distant nation abandoned to its fate.

He'd be back.

# 24

Now that Fares had completed his studies and graduated as a doctor, he needed to pause, calmly plan for the next stage, and set his priorities.

He wouldn't return to his homeland until he had accumulated enough funds to purchase a home, open his own clinic, and, in case his career took some time to get started, live a dignified life for a few years. He would not return to Beirut empty-handed, which meant he'd have to work in America for some years until he could return.

In the meantime, he also had to make the most of what he could gain from American civilization—and to transfer what was most necessary back to his homeland.

And he needed to seize the next opportunity to serve in the army, even if it was only for a year or for some months.

He would not return to his homeland carrying the memory of humiliation that he lived with because of his relationship with the American town girl, Jessie. He would erase this by making all those who conspired and plotted against him feel guilt and regret.

Fares bore no grudge toward anyone. But his personal and national dignity were at stake. He'd never forget that he'd left the American University of Beirut and emigrated to America for that very reason in the first place.

Besides, serving in the American army would make it easier for him to obtain American citizenship. That citizenship, in turn, would allow him to seek work in Beirut without pressure from the Ottoman authorities, thanks to the protection that foreign citizenship granted him throughout the empire. But finding work after graduating with a medical degree wasn't easy in general—and especially not in his particular case. First, he didn't have enough money to open up a private clinic. And, second, he was still a fresh graduate with no experience. No one would trust him yet. He wouldn't have even fully trusted himself.

The best path forward—as an initial step—was to start working as an assistant to a more experienced doctor. He started looking for the right opportunity, reading newspaper advertisements every morning in hopes of finding a suitable job.

Things went on like this for months. In the meantime, he asked for help from his father, whose own financial circumstances were far from favorable. He was on the verge of going back to work once again until one day, very early in the morning, he came across an ad seeking a medical assistant. He rushed to the listed address, hoping to be the first to arrive. But, to his disappointment, a crowd of new graduates had already made it there before him.

He considered not spending hours waiting in line, without real hope, and instead returning to his *káshshe* so as not to waste the day. But, to his surprise, the doctor asked him at the end of the interview to come back the next day for a second one.

"Do you know why I chose you out of all those excellent candidates?" the doctor asked him, after the second interview.

The question took Fares by surprise. He had been certain his selection was due to the strength of his file—clearly a fundamental requirement. Yet there were others whose files were just as impressive.

"I chose you for your name! 'Fares Hashem' doesn't sound American. And Americans trust doctors from faraway places. Women in particular tend to believe that foreign doctors have healing powers."

Fares was amazed by what he heard. Then he remembered that when he enrolled in medical school in St. Louis, he'd decided to Americanize his name to avoid racial prejudice. Yet something mysterious held him back. It was like a voice reaching him from Mount Lebanon, from his grandfather, his grandfather's grandfather, from the graveyards at the village's edge. So he kept his name.

His name *was* his connection to his country.

Fares Mansour Hashem would not meet his end on foreign soil—not even the United States of America, a country he held in the highest regard, a nation whose civilization he admired and whose laws he respected so deeply that he was determined to serve in its army.

And so Fares started working in a small American town of no more than a hundred people. It was a crossroads between several nearby towns, surrounded by fertile and prosperous farmland. Fares's job was to fill in for his employer, who only came in three days a week—Monday, Wednesday, and Friday—for an hour or two before noon. That was because his employer, the physician, owned other clinics in different locations.

The strange thing that happened to Fares was that the first person who came to seek his help was a farmer, tall and broad-shouldered with reddish hair and a pale face, whose skin was weathered by the sun.

"I have a dying calf!" the farmer exclaimed as he entered the clinic.

"A calf?" Fares replied in shock.

"Yes, a calf! I was told you're an Oriental, and I know Orientals know a lot about the mysteries of the world, about life and death."

Fares had to decline, reminding the man that he was a human doctor, not a veterinarian, and that the two fields of medicine were entirely different. By law, he had no right to intervene in areas beyond his specialization.

Fares's apology was extraordinarily polite. He feared that this farmer might be racist and hostile to foreigners in the town. Fares was the only newcomer to an area that had long been closed off to outsiders.

The first human case he encountered was a boy struggling for his life in his parents' home. Fares had to act right away. A priest was at the home when he arrived and had just completed the rites typically performed for someone near death. Fares couldn't save the boy, who died in his arms.

Before taking this job in that remote town, Fares hadn't treated a single patient. None of his professors had stood by his side to supervise him during his studies—nor was his employer with him. When Fares was in the last phase of his university studies, he wasn't allowed to treat anyone in the university hospital, unlike some of his American classmates who were given that opportunity. He suspected that the reason was political—or, in less diplomatic terms, racist.

The news spread through the village and its environs that the boy died at the hands of the new Syrian doctor, who was unable to do anything to save him. Consequently, Fares decided to leave the village and considered again Americanizing his name to something like "Jonathan" for his future job.

He was even preparing to return to New York and go back to work peddling, waiting for a better opportunity, when his employer arrived. He convinced Fares to change his mind and stay in the town. He told him that he knew that the boy who had died had a terminal illness—even his family knew it was incurable.

Fares agreed to give it another try, but before long his bad luck struck again. An even more serious case came to him: a woman with a weak heart who insisted on getting pregnant because she didn't yet have a child. She died in her fifth month, and it was "the Syrian doctor" who witnessed her final breath and her departure from life.

Once again Fares's boss tried to dissuade him from his firm decision to leave the village—but this time, he failed. The American physician, who managed clinics in various towns, then proposed that Fares swap posts with another doctor. Fares eventually agreed, persuaded after his boss told him that farmers living in remote villages rarely sought medical help unless the patient was already at death's door. He also told him that he had encountered many cases where the sick would die under his care.

He then demanded that Fares not change his name, reminding him that he had been chosen among others because of it. He assured him that bad phases could happen to any doctor, no matter their experience, and that this phase, too, would soon pass. Fares's successes in this new town soon began to unfold. The first case he faced was a young fifteen-year-old girl in a very critical position—and he healed her. Then came another difficult case, which he also managed to treat. He kept curing people until, within a few years, his reputation reached distant places. His appointments increased to the extent that some compared him to the second coming of Christ from the land of Palestine.

He attributed his success to conversing with patients and their families about the land of Palestine—about Bethlehem, the birthplace of Christ, Nazareth, where he lived with his parents, the Garden of Gethsemane, where he was arrested, and Jerusalem, where he was crucified. He'd tell them about the mountains of Lebanon surrounding Beirut, the villages scattered across it, along with the sacred cedar forests, pine trees, and oaks.

He would describe to them the plains of Syria and the hills of Palestine in a way that echoed the landscapes of Scripture. These American farmers and villagers, living in remote areas, loved hearing about the lands they had only read of in their holy book.

So it was that Fares decided to open a private clinic, once again postponing his return to Beirut. He felt guilty for not having fulfilled his promise to volunteer in the American army—but he hadn't given up hope yet.

The first person to visit Fares in his new clinic on Broadway—near the intersection with Grand Street, not far from his old residence—was Hasna, the girl from his village he had once planned to marry. She had quickly learned of his clinic's location and his start date. Word had spread fast among the Syrian-Lebanese community, who took pride in their dutiful son: now a respected doctor, admired by Americans for his skills, some even calling him a second Christ, coming from the land of Palestine.

"My health is fine," Hasna said to Fares. "But I came to tell you that my wedding is next week. If you still want to marry me, I'm ready to cancel everything and go with you—wherever, whenever."

Fares was caught off guard. Once again, he found himself breathing in the scent of the homeland through her. He rose and embraced her, trying to kiss her, but she pulled away. Her chastity only inflamed his desire, and when he tried to force himself on her, she resisted fiercely and pushed him off. Without a word of farewell, she stormed out of the clinic. The following week, she was married.

Fares thus postponed his return to Lebanon until he amassed a modest fortune. He deposited part of it in a bank, used another to buy shares, and spent the rest renting several apartments in New York City. But as his wealth grew—and the difficulty of returning to Lebanon with it—the longing only deepened: a yearning for the snow-capped mountains of his homeland, its tranquil sea, and the gentle breeze that carried solace to the ailing.

Then, burdened by guilt and the ache of yearning, he resolved to return for good to his homeland, to settle in Beirut, and to marry a local woman as soon as possible. This wouldn't be difficult; his fame preceded him there and had grown far beyond what it was in America. He arranged for his father to travel ahead of him to Beirut to purchase a house and secure a space for his clinic in the Ras Beirut neighborhood, near the American University. There, he hoped to offer a few courses, enabling him to stay connected with the younger generation and remain engaged with academic research. Ras Beirut—with its mix of sects and nationalities—appealed to him. He couldn't bear the thought of raising his children in a neighborhood marked by a single sectarian identity.

# 25

A year after his father's return, in 1898, while he was still in New York slowly selling off his properties and the shares he owned—careful not to rush and risk unnecessary losses—a war broke out between the United States and Spain in Cuba. American youth began volunteering in response to the homeland's call and in service of the beloved national flag. Fares saw no place for himself but among them, at the Broadway enlistment center. He volunteered as a physician until the war ended, fulfilling an old dream: to show the Americans who the Syrian truly was—that a Syrian could not only be a medical student and a professional, but a soldier as well.

Less than two weeks later, he received orders to set sail for Cuba aboard an American naval ship. The pleasant surprise was that, on the battlefield in Cuba, Fares discovered that there was a large number of Syrian volunteers in the American army, including Jibrael Elias Ward, from Tripoli!

"*Shú 'am tá'mel hawn?* What are you up to over here?" Fares asked him in Lebanese.

Jibrael responded to him in stumbling, broken English: "I come here to serve our magnificent flag . . . the stars and stripes . . . it is waving above the fortress of the freedom. I come here and contribute in the making for America her glorious history, full of progress, business, industry, and innovation. I am here to defend land of the enduring freedom, freedom that the Constitution protects her . . . Constitution give to every man his right."

Fares was stunned by this impassioned response, having expected nothing more than a brief introduction from Jibrael. He had no idea that the man had undergone a deeply troubling experience, one that clearly left its mark: Jibrael had been caught moving between tents and battalions in the encampment without explanation. He was accused of espionage because he looked more like a Spaniard than anyone else, on account of his darker complexion and facial features. To make matters worse, he spoke fluent Spanish—having lived for years in Argentina before immigrating to the United States.

The situation was only resolved when the commanding officer of his unit, who had previously served as police chief in Springfield, where Jibrael once lived, was able to vouch for him. He affirmed that Jibrael was "of Syrian, not of Spanish origins."

Fares the medic would later meet Jibrael the soldier near Colonel Theodore Roosevelt's tent on the outskirts of Santiago, Cuba. When the colonel fell ill and required medical attention, the now-famous Syrian doctor was summoned.

Colonel Roosevelt used to keep Jibrael close at hand, relying on him to serve as a Spanish translator whenever the need arose.

What a coincidence!

Fares was astonished when he laid eyes on Colonel Roosevelt. It was the same face he'd seen in Beirut near the American University in the early 1870s. News had spread that an important American figure, a Roosevelt, would visit Beirut with his family and stay at the home of the president of the university, Dr. Bliss. So Fares and his friends Jurji and Saadeddine went to the university and watched the young Theodore ride a donkey with Bliss's son, meandering around the area and laughing. At one point, Theodore nearly fell off the donkey's back and brought Bliss's son down with him.

"Yes, indeed!" the colonel answered when Fares asked him. "I visited Beirut, and I loved it—I loved your country. It holds a special place in my heart. I approved your deployment as soon as I learned where you come from. I enlisted the help of my translator, Jibrael, for the same reason."

In that far-flung land, Fares nearly fainted with joy upon hearing this account.

Jibrael informed him, speaking English so the colonel would understand, that several Syrian army volunteers were currently on Cuban soil. Fares was pleased: The way he saw it, these soldiers were gaining combat experience with modern, state-of-the-art methods, and they would become the vanguard of the future Syrian army—or of Lebanon, at least. At the time, it had begun to appear that three states would arise in Ottoman Syria (Syria, Lebanon, and Palestine), rather than one. Whenever Fares saw Jibrael, he'd advise him to be a paragon of good conduct and virtue, to give a positive impression of Syrian troops on the battlefield. So he was angered one day when he caught Jibrael selling rations to the troops. What happened was that Jibrael had taken an unnecessary pair of trousers with him to Cuba, tied the legs together into a makeshift saddlebag, and began filling it with leftover rations that had been distributed among the soldiers and left behind. In the evening when the troops were resting, Jibrael would move between them and sell them the cans. In a single day of business—the day after they'd disembarked the steamships on the Cuban coast—he earned sixty dollars.

When Fares heard about this, he told him, "America is a good country. Don't forget to return the favor."

Another time, Fares watched Jibrael ask an American named Farrar Whitman for a cigarette shortly before they reached the town of El Caney. Jibrael, like most of the other soldiers in his company, had run out of tobacco, so Farrar claimed that all he had left was this cigarette in his hand, which he was smoking with great relish. But Jibrael caught him some time later hiding behind a tree trunk rolling a cigarette, using a bag he'd pulled out of his shirt pocket.

Jibrael walked up to him without hesitation. "Your trick's not working on me anymore," he declared. "Now give me cigarette!"

"I wouldn't give my own father a cigarette even if he came all the way from Springfield," Farrar said. "In conditions like these, cigarettes are the most valuable thing I have."

Jibrael, who was intensely craving a cigarette, admitted to Fares that he hoped this man would get killed so he could take his cigarette box. Fares became wary of Jibrael, worried that his friend might be ill-natured.

His fears were reinforced by what he witnessed in the initial hours of the famous battle for the town of El Caney, mere miles from Santiago, which the Spaniards had fortified with cavalry and infantry, rows of trenches and rapid-fire cannons. Jibrael's muscles tensed up as he lay prone on the ground when the shelling and gunfire erupted. He began to tremble with fear, as if the rifle he held were no more than a club. Each time a grenade was thrown from their side or the Spaniards lobbed one toward them, he clung to the earth more tightly. Things got worse when he turned to his right and saw one of his comrades thrashing around covered in blood, so Jibrael began firing at random without aiming. Fares approached him when he saw his friend frozen.

"*Yá Jibrael*!" Fares shouted, addressing him in classical Arabic. "*Ánta jundíyun súri: qátil min ájli wátanik! Amríka l-ána híya súriya*! You are a Syrian soldier, so fight for your homeland! Right now, America is Syria!"

After this initial panic, Jibrael pulled himself together anew and proved himself to be a brave soldier. He advanced and charged, narrowly escaping death multiple times. His display of courage astonished his American comrades and impressed his superior officers. The officer that had accused him of espionage was embarrassed to face him after witnessing such a degree of bravery and efficiency in combat, and he apologized profusely.

Fares watched as Jibrael advanced from position to position, toward the fortified lines the Spanish held at the gates of El Caney. Soldiers were collapsing dead all around him, filling him with resolve and momentum. Jibrael's fear and wariness transformed into true glory. But at one point Fares spotted him as he crouched over a mortally wounded soldier, took a smoking box from the man's pocket, rolled a cigarette, and smoked it. Fares, exasperated by what he'd seen, asked him about it during a rest period.

Jibrael smiled and replied, in Lebanese Arabic, "*Ma bádda hal ádd*—it's not worth it!" What he meant was that it didn't deserve so much attention, that Fares should take things more lightly—not with such seriousness and solemnity.

"Americans love pranks and jokes!" Jibrael added. "Where's the harm in what I did?"

Fares didn't treat the wounds Jibrael suffered during that battle because he only found out Jibrael had been wounded the following day. As soon as he found out, he rushed over to see him and found a nurse by his side who was looking after him with great care. Despite the pain, Jibrael was in good spirits. He was so pleased with the nurse that he nearly forgot he'd been injured. It came as a surprise to him that a young woman not even twenty years old was lifting him with both hands, examining him and turning him over, empathizing with him and apologizing when she caused him pain, as if he were a precious pearl in front of her—all with the utmost innocence and purity.

This young American volunteer nurse was deeply grateful for this Syrian who'd come from far away, who was defying death to defend her country. She felt that no matter what she did for him, it wouldn't be enough. Jibrael had never experienced anything like this situation before. Never had a woman gotten so close to him and touched him without reluctance or awkwardness—a respectable young woman, younger than twenty, no less. He'd never felt he was such an important person. Jibrael told Fares in Arabic that he couldn't believe how well this nurse was treating him. With a smile blending embarrassment and mischievousness, he also informed Fares that he'd sometimes become aroused in this situation and was ashamed she'd notice what was going on below the waist. Once, he even climaxed while she was cleaning his wounds.

Fares admonished him to get hold of himself, "lest we come across as an unsophisticated people." He proceeded to reiterate something Jibrael had learned years prior: that women are free in this country, that it was not a sign of depravity or ill intent for women to mingle with men, and that women here work in all fields, particularly in nursing.

"The nurse taking care of you right now is tending to dozens of injured soldiers, if not hundreds," Fares explained. "She's as proud as can be to serve a country that punishes wrongdoers and delivers the persecuted, a country that adorns its territory with the banners of freedom and progress, a country whose darkness is illuminated by the shining stars on its fluttering flag."

"Okay, okay!" Jibrael implored, fed up with the moralizing lecture.

Three days after Jibrael's injury, the army leadership transported the wounded on a military steamship to Key West, Florida, accompanied by a contingent that included Dr. Fares. Among the wounded was another Syrian from Zahle called Hanna Haddad, who had Americanized his name as "John Head." He had an eye injury that could have led to blindness, but his spirits were very high. He was unconcerned about his future, as the American government hadn't let him down at any point. He had an operation at the army hospital in Atlanta, where they'd been transported aboard a Red Cross train. John managed to keep his eye.

Despite Fares's satisfaction with Jibrael as a soldier in combat, the latter caused him a good deal of vexation, as he was in an entirely different mood and mentality.

As they rode the train to Richmond, Virginia, Fares noticed that Jibrael had burned holes in his army cap with his cigarette. When Fares asked why he'd done that, Jibrael responded that he hadn't been paying attention and that it had happened by mistake. At the station, the authorities organized a warm reception befitting the "Heroes of Cuba," as they were called. A large crowd was in attendance, and there was an elaborate spread. Suddenly, a girl around sixteen years old approached and asked Jibrael for permission to feed him. His mind was blown from the surprise.

"I can see your hand's injured," she said, "so would you mind if I feed you?"

When he claimed that his other hand had rheumatism, she effused even more compassion for him and sat beside him to feed him. Jibrael wished he had the stomach of the whale that swallowed the Prophet Jonah. Fares looked on, amazed by what he saw, and his appreciation deepened for American civilization. He grew simultaneously annoyed at Jibrael's behavior. "*Zéda*—now he's overdone it," Fares said to himself, "exploiting the credulity and gratitude of the Americans!"

One of the onlookers approached Jibrael. "Looks like your cap fought in the battle, too—and got injured like you did!" the man remarked. "Would you sell it to me? I'll give you whatever you like."

Jibrael claimed that it would be difficult for him to part with it, because it had sentimental value, and he wanted to keep it as a souvenir. The man fell silent and began to walk away. Worried he'd lose the opportunity, Jibrael quickly added, "But if you really want it, then take it."

The man was overjoyed and paid him twenty-five dollars.

Then Jibrael convinced another soldier on the train to sell him his cap for five dollars. He took it and made several holes in it with a cigarette so it looked like he'd narrowly survived. He sold that one, too.

But then he became quite sad: None of the other wounded soldiers would agree to sell him their hats.

"Maybe that's because they found out about your little business," Fares told him. "Maybe they don't want any part in it!"

He wished Jibrael would put an end to this enterprise. It could undermine the good will he had gained from his bravery in the war—or, worse yet, give a negative impression of Syrian soldiers. But Jibrael lacked the disposition of his countryman, the refined, educated doctor.

Whenever Americans asked Jibrael what happened to their deceased son, he'd answer that he had personally buried him. When a rich man asked him about his son, Jibrael answered that he and three other soldiers had carried his son to his grave and buried him. The man gave Jibrael some money and promised to give him more if he managed to provide the addresses of the other three soldiers.

More importantly, the mother and sister of Farrar Whitman came to see him at the hospital in Springfield and asked him to tell them what happened to their son in detail. He told them that Farrar entrusted him with passing on his last words to his parents. To prove it, he gave them the box Farrar used to put his tobacco in—which Jibrael had stolen. The two women burst into tears. They offered him a token of gratitude in the form of a watch and a gold chain. Even more than that, Farrar's father, who owned the region's most significant newspaper, published a call for monetary donations and managed to collect some $470 for Jibrael.

The Syrian expatriates held a crowded reception for him. Passionate words were spoken, in prose and in verse. Jibrael would later go on to found associations along the lines of the Young Turks, but with the aim of liberating all the Syrian lands and establishing a state on the American model.[1]

1. The Young Turks were a Turkish nationalist reform movement formed in Ottoman Anatolia at the end of the nineteenth century. The movement initially emerged in response to the illiberal measures of the antepenultimate sultan Abdülhamid II (r. 1876–1909), including his suspension of the constitution in 1878, a mere two years after its promulgation.

# 26

Fares, on the other hand, returned to Cuba to resume his service. He remained there for several months of combat until a truce was declared. Around that time, he met a Chinese girl. She was living with a Lebanese woman in her fifties who owned a modest house near the location where his company was stationed.

The woman came from a village in the south of what is today Lebanon. When she was a child, her parents were killed during an instance of the sectarian warfare that afflicts Lebanon periodically. She and her brother, who was one year younger, were raised by her grandmother after they moved to Beirut and the latter began working as a maid.

When she turned sixteen, she and her brother migrated to Cuba, where some relatives from the village had already gone. They settled near El Caney after purchasing a parcel of land, which they'd cultivate to survive. Her brother died suddenly a bachelor, leaving his sister all alone: She, too, hadn't married, in anticipation of her return to Lebanon.

The Chinese girl found herself at this Syrian woman's house after a long journey from one place and form of suffering to the next. The two took a liking to one another and became as close as sisters. The Chinese girl spoke both Spanish and English and used to insist she'd made her living only by working in houses—never through the sin of prostitution. Her Lebanese counterpart didn't ask about her history: There was nothing for her to verify. All that mattered was that the girl was there and they got along as if she were a sister or cousin from Mount Lebanon. The woman was well aware of the things migrants—especially women—have to face.

The girl, Sawa, was beautiful, which made her more fearful of the soldiers—the Spaniards, first of all, and the Americans, secondly—even though Chinese women were not very desirable to American men at the time. Most of them were brought to America to work among the Chinese laborers, whom white prostitutes refused to serve.

The Lebanese woman, Flora, wasted no time before hiding Sawa when she saw that Spanish troops had arrived and were fortifying their positions. Sawa only went outside when she was sure nobody was around.

One day after the Americans occupied the town, Flora heard someone speaking Arabic with a Lebanese accent:

"*Shémem ríht tabbouleh*! I smell tabbouleh!"

Her hair stood up: She was actually chopping parsley for a plate of tabbouleh! Trembling, she moved closer to the source of the sound. She hadn't heard anyone speaking Arabic in a long time. She saw Fares in his uniform. There was another soldier with him, a Syrian from a village high up Mount Lebanon.

"*Éntu ulád 'arab?*" she called out to them in Lebanese Arabic. "Are you Arabs?"

She took off toward them, embraced them, and invited them to her house. Flora had recognized them based on the color of their skin and hair, their height, the way they spoke, their glances and gestures. She didn't think, she didn't hesitate—and she wasn't wrong.

She soon called Sawa, who came out of her hiding place and greeted them with a wave, speaking English.

Fares was familiar with many stories about the Chinese. He knew some of them were accurate and others racist propaganda. He also knew a lot about Chinese women, and he was not under the impression that any Chinese woman living away from her family must necessarily be a prostitute. As for Flora, the Arab woman, she appeared scarcely different from his own mother or his female relatives. Flora had hispanicized her name, which in Arabic was Zahra (meaning "flower").

Fares was convinced that Sawa wasn't a prostitute, even though she wasn't a virgin when he slept with her the first time. She let him do it with little hesitation, but he was caught off guard when she asked him to embrace her after he was satisfied. His friend, the other Lebanese, tried to make a move on her, but she flatly refused and buried herself in Flora's embrace, quivering. When Fares tried to convince her—as an experiment—to sleep with his friend, she erupted in tears, nearly choking as she sobbed. It took him aback.

The next time he was with her, she asked him just to hold her. She hoped he'd be content with that. At that moment, Fares felt he'd become very close to her. He was glad just to hold her, and they stayed like that for a long time, like lovers.

Then Sawa stopped letting Fares sleep with her. He complied with her wishes ungrudgingly, and they'd lie next to each other chatting for as long as his time permitted. Sawa told him she wasn't a prostitute, and, even if she were, she wouldn't have concealed that from him. He believed her in a heartbeat and assured her he would accept her as a life partner, as the mother of his children, even if she had been a prostitute—just so long as no one found out about that.

Sawa began to wait patiently for him, with bated breath, each time he went to work as a medic behind the front lines. It unsettled her whenever she heard cannonfire coming from one direction or another.

Flora was very pleased with their relationship. But at the same time she was worried that Sawa would go with Fares to New York or someplace else and leave her all alone. And she was right. When the war ended and Fares was discharged, he asked the chaplain to marry them, and she returned to New York with him.

But Fares encouraged Flora to come home to Lebanon and live with them in Beirut, or down the street from them. He convinced her to follow his lead, sell her possessions, and come home instead of dwelling on her sorrows all alone in this foreign land. She agreed.

"Cuba's given me a lot," she said. "But I'm dying of homesickness."

Flora asked him to stay in touch and let her know when he'd arrived and gotten settled in Lebanon, so she could catch up to him right away.

Bidding her farewell, Sawa assured her, "I'll be the link between you two—don't worry!"

# 27

Fares and his wife, Sawa, spent a year in New York. During that time, he was able to obtain American citizenship with little difficulty and made active preparations for the return to Beirut.

Fares felt accomplished. He wanted to reap the fruits of this success for the benefit of the homeland.

He then sold what he wished to sell fairly easily. He gathered his things, and the two boarded a steamship heading eastward—toward the Star of the Mediterranean: Beirut.

Before setting sail, Fares wrote to his father with the date of their arrival. He also wrote to his close friends, especially Jurji in Cairo and Saadeddine in Beirut. Both of them replied that they'd be waiting for him at the harbor, which meant that Jurji would leave his work in Cairo, where he'd become a prominent figure, and arrive in Beirut ahead of Fares.

Fares and Sawa's plan was to spend two weeks in Paris, a week in Marseille, and another week in Rome and Naples before ending their journey in Beirut. The Atlantic Ocean was generally calm for the twenty days it took them to cross it and reach Le Havre, France. They were in first class, naturally. Sawa was thrilled.

They talked a great deal. She loved listening to him tell her about Beirut, about Lebanon's mountains that envelop the city, about Jerusalem and timeless Damascus. He loved listening to her tell him about herself and what little she knew about China.

Sawa had never been to China, but her parents used to tell her about it. They managed to escape death in San Francisco in the summer of 1877, when unrest against Chinese laborers reached its height on July 23rd. Bands of young American men began roaming the streets. They burned the houses and shops of the Chinese and killed them with knives and bullets, or hanged them from trees and poles.

That night, an American couple offered them protection, hiding her parents until things had subsided.

As Fares listened intently to these stories, he compared the torment her family and other Chinese immigrants continued to endure with what he, his family, and other immigrants from Syria had faced. The suffering of the Syrians, inhuman as it had it been, paled in comparison to that of the Chinese.

"Evil knows no limits!" he remarked as they sat on the deck of the ship one quiet, beautiful day.

Sawa told him her father had fled to Cuba from Peru, where he used to work on a plantation. He participated in the unrest of 1870, which began when a group of desperate Chinese attacked a plantation owner and three of his dinner guests, butchered them, and desecrated their bodies.

The spark spread to other Chinese laborers in and around the city, who set off slaughtering any men they encountered, raping the women before killing them. They hung up the bodies of their victims, naked or in whatever clothes they had on, from street posts. But the next city over was prepared and caught the laborers by surprise before they arrived, killing many of them and littering the roads with their bodies.

Sawa was certain that her father had been one of the mutineers who had raped and murdered, though he never mentioned it: he always claimed he'd survived by defending himself. He told her a lot about the torment he faced from the time he boarded the ship on the Chinese coast until arriving in Peru.

"A quarter of us died, and they were thrown overboard into the sea before we reached the shores of Peru," her father related to her. "None of them were buried in their villages, among their ancestors, for people to pay their respects—and no one ever will until the end of time.

"When we arrived, we were greeted on the shore by whips made from dried bull muscle. The first time I was whipped, by a man on horseback, I yanked on the whip and he fell off his horse. It was a disaster. It wasn't just me who was punished: They lashed everyone on board the ship all day long. Then they cut our braided hair, our distinctive queues that we once prided ourselves on.[1]

"They undressed us so the planters could assess our physical strength before they bought us. We used to perform unbelievable tasks for twenty-one hours a day. When I first arrived, my job was loading ships with manure. The stench constantly had me close to suffocating. They stationed guards between us and the sea so we couldn't commit suicide by throwing ourselves into the water, out of sheer exhaustion and injustice. Once, I distracted the guards and plunged into the water, clutching a pot full of manure so I'd sink. But they caught me and punished me, throwing me in a water tank without food, with my arms and legs shackled. They affixed a wooden ring around my neck to keep me from drowning.

"Then one of the landowners came and hired me through the agent who'd brought me to Peru. I was happy to get away from the stench, but life was not easier in my new place of work. I used to dream of drowning in the sea, but then I began to dream of hanging myself from a tree . . .

"They fed us only enough to keep us alive. When people fell ill, they were taken far away and shot like rats to keep from stirring anyone's sympathy or disgust."

"Evil is boundless!" Fares reiterated, pulling her into an embrace. Unable to keep her secret any longer, Sawa confessed to the unthinkable: In that moment, she wished to bare herself before him entirely.

"I am not my father's daughter," she revealed. "When my father met my mother, she was pregnant. She'd fled San Francisco after the agent who brought her over from China to work in houses tried to force her into prostitution, because American prostitutes refused to serve Chinese clients. There were tens of thousands of young Chinese men without their wives, and there weren't enough Chinese prostitutes to meet the demand.

"When my mother refused to do it, the agent raped her to force her to accept his offer. Again she refused. By the time she reached Cuba, her

1. The queue is a men's hairstyle where the front half of the head is shaven, and the remaining hair is grown long and braided. The Qing dynasty issued an edict in 1645 mandating that male subjects adopt the queue, which came to symbolize Han Chinese identity.

belly was round. But my father told her, 'Forget about it. Consider what's in your belly mine.'"

Fares had a hard time accepting all this. But he calmed down once he learned that Sawa hadn't told anyone, not even Flora. He asked her to forget about it and not to mention it to anyone, especially in Beirut.

Later, Sawa told him that ever since her parents died she'd dreamt of burying a memento of them—a lock of hair and fingernail clippings from each of them—in her father's village in China.

A week before the ship reached France, Sawa told Fares:

"I think I'm pregnant!"

Fares was thrilled at the news. To celebrate, they opened a bottle of champagne, as the French do. Then they counted the days since Sawa last had her period, counted again, and discovered that a month and a half had gone by.

Fares and the newly expectant Sawa roamed the streets of Le Havre, where the ship from New York had moored. They wandered the sidewalks, underneath arches and between columns. Fares searched for the French clerk who had helped him during his short stay in the city as he prepared to cross the ocean to America. But Fares couldn't find him. He discovered that the place where the man used to work had become a restaurant, which left him melancholy. All at once, Fares felt how long it had been. Time flies, no matter how difficult or slow the days may be. Sixteen years had gone by like a reverie.

They went on to have an enjoyable time in Paris, the city of theaters, galleries, and libraries; of medical schools and hospitals; of labor movements; of secularism—*laïcité*—and the separation of church and state. This city that loved and took care of itself, that took pleasure in breaking free of all limitations, looked more beautiful and more lustrous with each passing day.

Sawa adored Paris, even though her striking Chinese features attracted attention wherever she went. But she was used to that.

Anywhere she went, the Parisians called her *madame*. Anywhere her husband went, they called him *monsieur*. Sawa liked these words and the French language. She memorized some phrases and vocabulary and resolved to learn French to fluency in Beirut, where many educated Lebanese spoke it.

They visited the Eiffel Tower, then the Arc de Triomphe at the Place de l'Étoile. They cruised down the Seine in a rowboat and passed by the Cathédrale Notre Dame, the setting of the novel *The Hunchback of Notre Dame*, which Fares had read in French before he left Lebanon for America, then saw as a play in English in New York.

Fares told Sawa the story of the hunchback, which moved her deeply.

At the Louvre, Fares saw young schoolchildren gathered in a circle around their teacher, who was explaining artifacts that had been brought from the East.

"*Máta ya biládi?*" he sighed.

*Country of mine, when will the time come?*

At the museum, Fares saw men and women of all ages contemplating the displays. His life circumstances in New York hadn't permitted him to soak in the culture as he'd wished. It wasn't every day that he'd have the chance to visit Paris, the capital of culture, so he sought to take advantage of his time there as much as possible.

During their visit, Fares and Sawa stayed on the Rive Gauche (the left bank of the Seine) in the Latin Quarter, near the campus of the Sorbonne. They took walks down to the Seine and sat at riverfront cafés. There, Fares met several Lebanese who were studying in Paris or on their way to or from the Americas. He had long discussions with many of those he met about matters of the homeland, especially Beirut, about projects that had been carried out there before and after his migration and those that ought to be completed. Fares was still an infant when work had been completed on the Beirut-Damascus Highway and the first carts since Roman times, over 1,800 years before, rolled along the road. The road, which reduced travel times between the two cities by more than half, had room for horse-drawn carriages that transported people and goods. Glass became commonplace in Beirut, and windows and doors were widened. No longer did one encounter windows that weren't made of glass—no longer did houses have narrow openings, like they used to.

Security ruled the day. Many roads were paved and filled up with carriages, day and night. The main roads were illuminated, water was delivered to people's homes through metal pipes, and the harbor was modernized. Many universities and schools opened. Mail and telegraph services connected Beirut to a communications network spanning the whole world. The railroads were extended between Beirut and Damascus, making Beirut the port of the Levant and the entire Syrian interior. Newspapers and assorted periodicals proliferated, with Egypt close by for those who wished to write freely or to work in politics. The city became replete with restaurants, cafés, hotels, and businesses, along with a multitude of agents who represented foreign companies. The population of Beirut doubled to two hundred thousand, and all signs pointed to the city becoming the official capital of Lebanon—which was to break away from Syria and Palestine and become a state in its own right.

(No one expected that this country would one day endure the horrors it has endured. No one could have imagined that its people would be subjected to the perennial wars and calamities they have weathered.)

# 28

The last thing Fares said to Sawa gave no indication that anything was amiss. He told her he was craving a plate of raw *kibbeh* with lots of olive oil, onion, and mint. Sawa knew what he meant because he often used to tell her about Lebanese food and the dishes he loved and craved. She had learned a bit about the cuisine from living with Flora, so she promised him she'd be the best cook in all of Syria.

And so it was: Fares expressed a strong desire for a plate of *kibbeh nayyeh* with lots of oil, onion, and mint.

Then he fell silent.

Dead.

This was on the train, shortly before they reached Marseille.

He hadn't been able to tell her about the sudden heaviness he felt in his chest, which made it hard to breathe—or about how things had suddenly collapsed and lost their form.

Sawa called out to onlookers and tried as best she knew how to resuscitate him. But it was no use. After it dawned on her that he was dead, she wrapped him in a blanket and sat beside him, gazing out the window of her compartment and ruminating on destiny. She wept in silence, in dignity, until the train pulled into the station in Marseille.

In the few hours before reaching the station, Sawa had to make a crucial decision. Should she bury him in Marseille and go back to New York alone? Or should she have the body prepared so she could bring him with her to the Port of Beirut, then bury him among the graves of his ancestors?

Where was she to give birth to the child in her belly?

Sawa had already made her decision when the train reached Marseille: She'd proceed directly to Beirut without stopping in Rome and

Naples. She wasn't afraid to approach her husband's family—awaiting the arrival of a doctor who could raise the dead, whose fame had spread far and wide—with his body in tow. It didn't worry her to travel by herself, next to a corpse and with a fetus in her belly, nor that she didn't know any Arabic or understand the customs of the distant East. She wanted to be true to Fares's dream of returning home.

Sawa didn't write to let his family know what'd happened to their loved one, or to tell them about her arrival in Beirut ahead of time. She was going to arrive in Beirut sooner than any letter could.

She resolved to take the first steamship to Beirut and, naturally, to cancel the trip to Italy she'd planned with her husband. She would work matters out as best she could when she got there. She knew the names of his father, his siblings, and some of his relatives. And she knew their addresses as written on the letters Fares used to receive from them.

Sawa visited him several times a day, in the dark corner where he'd been placed on the deck of the ship. She prayed for him, in her own way: She hadn't been brought up within any tradition, nor did she follow a particular religion.

How strongly it pained her that she couldn't see the Mediterranean through his eyes, the way he'd described it to her so many times.

The waters of the sea weren't a brilliant blue like he'd told her. Quite the opposite: They were terrifying—and alluring!

Yes, alluring!

But there was no power on Earth that could have tempted Sawa to take her life at sea. Not when she carried a part of Fares in her belly.

In those days, the Port of Beirut was unable to receive large steamships like the one Sawa was traveling on, so small boats would act as water taxis, ferrying passengers and goods from the ships anchored far from the wharf. This was new to Sawa. Everything was new. She didn't have any idea what was going on when the water taxi operators began fighting over her and the coffin with her husband's body inside. Amid all the chaos and commotion, she was loaded into one boat and the coffin into another, competing boat. So she screamed with all her might, in whatever language and using whatever words came to her. She nearly fell into the water so as not to let the coffin out of her sight. The few minutes that separated her from the beach felt like an eternity. But, in the end, her husband's coffin arrived at the exact same time she did.

Then she asked the porters to place the coffin in a secluded place. She stood next to it, waiting for the travelers to leave and activity to die down on the wharf to see what she could do.

The ship had arrived around noon in November. The weather was clear and the temperature very mild.

It was at that moment that Kamal Manat, a port interpreter who worked at the port, happened to pass by and spotted this foreign woman with her striking and unusual features, standing perplexed next to a coffin. He approached her and asked what she was doing—first in French, then they quickly switched to English. She told him what had happened, and he realized that the name of her husband, which she pronounced in her own way, sounded familiar to him . . . wasn't it that famous doctor?

Kamal promised her he'd ask after Fares's family and come back to her as soon as possible. He advised her to set down the coffin somewhere and to relax in the waiting room. He helped her move the coffin into a quiet, sequestered corner, then left her in the waiting room after telling the official in charge of the area to look after her.

It was obvious that Kamal should have first sought out Fares's friends and acquaintances from the American University, students and faculty, to inform them of the passing of Dr. Fares Hashem—the famous physician who lived abroad in America, who used to be a student at the university, then completed his specialization in the United States—and to ask them about his family and relatives.

The poor bastard had no idea what was likely to come of his inquiries.

Three students who'd caught wind of the matter wasted no time to hatch a plot and put it into action. One of them was sent to lead Kamal Manat to the home of Fares's family in Saifi near Beirut (and today located in the heart of Beirut). The other two hired a horse cart, whose driver they trusted, and set off for the port.

The employee on duty, whom Kamal had asked to look after this foreign lady, played his part exactly as he was told. At the right moment, he called out to her and engaged her at length in conversation. He had no language skills—not even classical Arabic, which he struggled to read. He only knew how to speak the local dialect he'd grown up with. Still, he trapped her there standing in front of him for a long time—long enough for the two students to load the coffin onto the cart and take it to the sea under cover of darkness, which had just fallen. They took out the body and dug a hole, where they buried the empty coffin. Then they dressed the corpse in a fresh *khawája* outfit, complete with a European-style hat. They placed a lit cigar in its mouth and sat it upright in the cart between them, propping it up from both sides. They took it into the American University through the eastern entrance, known today as the Medical Gate.

Once Sawa managed to break free of this employee's endless interrogation, she hurried to visit Fares and "tell him" what happened.

But she couldn't find him.

She went back to the complicit employee straight away and dragged him by the hand to the spot. But he kept pretending not to understand anything, until Sawa began to scream.

She was aware of the theft of bodies in Beirut. Fares had told her what he and his friends used to do when they were students to keep the medical school open. But it never occurred to her that he himself would suffer such a fate.

"My husband!" she shrieked in English. "Where is my husband?!"

But the hall was empty—and what good was a scream swallowed up by the din of crashing waves?

Finally Kamal the interpreter arrived. He'd made his way, accompanied by one of the students, to the home of Fares Ibrahim. They'd already wasted a great deal of precious time searching—which, of course, was a student "guide's" job. Kamal had also spent a long while figuring out the right way to inform the family gently of Fares's death. He first told them he'd encountered a woman at the port with Chinese features who said she was Fares's wife. As they made their way to the port, he revealed that she had a coffin with her, which held the body of Fares, who'd died on the train from Paris to Marseille.

He used this gradual approach so the news didn't blindside them.

"My husband!" Sawa continued to shout by the time Abu Fares looked around from afar. He heard her yelling and, because he spoke English, immediately understood what she was saying. But he thought she was simply mourning the loss of her husband, not of the coffin that held his body. He rushed over to her and called her by name.

"Sawa!" he called out, rushing over to her. "I'm Fares's father!"

He pulled her close, and she slipped into his arms and began to sob. Then the aunts and women neighbors in attendance began to wail and shriek when they saw Mansour hugging his strange-looking Chinese daughter-in-law.

All of them wanted to see the coffin so they could weep for the deceased. But they couldn't find it. They looked everywhere, utterly baffled. By the time they reached the corner where the coffin had been, Sawa had managed to explain to Mansour what had happened. At first he couldn't comprehend what he'd heard. But soon everything made sense. Fares, still a student in Beirut, had told him about the issue of dissection and cadavers at the university.

# 29

The first person Abu Fares contacted was Officer Saadeddine al-Jabawi, whose close friendship with his son he was well aware of. He'd visited Saadeddine as soon as he reached Beirut on his way back from New York and gave him a letter from Fares. Abu Fares also knew that the two had an ongoing correspondence. Saadeddine immediately set off to lead a patrol, which established a perimeter around the university's eastern entrance, the medical gate, and prepared an ambush for the cart that carried the body.

But the cart carrying Fares's body entered the medical school before the patrol could arrive.

The ambush had been set up outside. Inside, the students—summoned from the library, the dormitories, and their recreation areas—were dividing up the corpse. Each of them began dissecting their divided portion under their professor's supervision. Cadavers were dissected as soon as they arrived so there was absolutely no possibility of retrieving the body—no hope whatsoever for the family or for anyone else.

The guard stationed at the eastern gate saw a cart with its driver, two students, and a man sitting between them dressed like a European, wearing a hat like foreigners did and with a lit cigar in his mouth.

The guard told them that had it occurred to him to inspect this foreigner sitting in the middle, perhaps he'd have noticed the discoloration.

Officer Saadeddine knew how these things worked. He knew what happened to the bodies that were reported missing. Sometimes he turned a blind eye to it. He was a supporter of the university, and he continued to do what he could to help out.

But everything had its limits. The body of such an esteemed man deserved respect!

There had already been much trepidation about the theft of bodies in Beirut before Fares's body was stolen. But it was this event—the broad daylight theft of a doctor's body from the wharf, the body of a man known for performing miracles—that left Beirutis deeply afraid: afraid for their dead, their sick, their children, and anyone alone at night. Women spent long periods at the cemeteries to visit the graves of parents, children, and relatives who were recently interred until the bodies had broken down. Men began to accompany them on many occasions after rumors spread that some of the women used the visits as a pretext to meet men.

The volume of hearsay in the city about stolen bodies was immeasurable.

There were stories about bodies being stolen in Cairo and Istanbul. Both cities had medical schools.

At the time, there was also talk of what had happened in Edinburgh in 1827. Two men, Burke and Hare, killed sixteen people and sold their bodies to a professor of anatomy. This bloodbath went on for a full year. If their crimes hadn't come to light following the murder of a woman who came from the countryside to look for her son, the two would've continued. Every child in Beirut in those days knew the names Burke and Hare and had heard exactly how they carried out their crimes. Hare blocked the woman's airway while Burke pressed down on her chest until she died, leaving her body unscathed.

Anatomy professors everywhere in the world wanted cadavers in perfect condition.

Saadeddine was unable to get his hands on his friend's body despite being certain that it was in the morgue at the medical school of the American University. Or perhaps it was at the medical school of the Jesuit University that'd been founded a few years prior—but that university, it appeared, had its own ways and means.

It was a very simple matter for Saadeddine to ascertain the body's location. All he had to do was reconstruct the sequence of events and ask Kamal, the port interpreter, whom it was that he'd spoken to. Kamal, angry with his friends, was about to lash out and give up their names. But he held back.

It would've been easy for Saadeddine to ask Kamal who he spent time with, who his friends were.

But he already knew enough!

He knew enough because not a single body had ever been returned from the medical school since the theft of bodies had come into fashion—in other words, since the medical school opened. Given the circumstances, all Saadeddine could do was bring Abu Fares and Sawa to the house Abu Fares had bought for his son to live in with his family—and assure them they should never hesitate to ask for his help.

Jurji Zaidan, who'd arrived from Cairo to meet his friend Fares at the port some days later, was horrified by the news. He immediately met with Saadeddine, and, after some discussion, the two reached the same conclusion. Saadeddine agreed to end the search for the body.

Here ended the journey of Fares Mansour Hashem in the life of this world. But Sawa's journey hadn't ended yet.

She was pregnant: Where was she going to give birth?

# 30

Just as Sawa had no reservations about going with Fares all the way to the homeland he adored and dreamt of returning to, so, too, was she decisive in that moment. When the family had finished accepting condolences about a week later, her father-in-law, Mansour, came to her.

"Make any decision you wish," he told her, "and I promise to carry it out. If you want to go back to America, you can do so whenever you like. If you want to return to your parents' country, you can. All the riches my son earned belong to you and your child."

He'd barely finished speaking when she answered that her decision was to stay there, in Beirut—to live in her husband's house, in his country, with his son or daughter whom she'd deliver in about seven months.

Sawa gave birth to a son. She named him Fares after his father.

The beautiful Sawa came to love her life in Beirut. She was a vigorous worker, successful in business, and her wealth multiplied.

She grew accustomed to the people who came from everywhere to marvel at her. She became used to the neighborhood kids crowding around her when they saw her. At first it annoyed her, but with time she acclimated. She figured out what streets to traverse and at what times of day, whom to associate with and whom not to, how and where to mingle with people. She came to know the lay of the land and the ambience of the city.

Still, many things were said about her. Beirut couldn't believe that such a beautiful and wealthy woman could reject the advances of famous men. A rumor spread that Djemal Pasha the Turk, dubbed *al-saffáh*—"the Butcher"—by Lebanese and Syrians, who besieged Mount Lebanon during World War I and caused a famine that eliminated a quarter of its population, had spent time alone with her.[1] They said she'd become pregnant thereafter, and that this was why she'd migrated to China to give birth and leave her child with relatives. People also said this child grew up to become one of Mao Zedong's aides and was friends with George Hatem, a Lebanese American doctor who had close ties to the chairman.[2]

Then Fares, son of Sawa, had a child whom he named Mansour, after his paternal grandfather. That was around 1925.

Then Mansour had a son in 1951, whom he named Jawan after the son of the *gházal* poet 'Umar bin Abi Rabi'a.[3]

This Jawan was the one who said, "I'm sick of living in a country made up of Muslims and Christians: Sunnis, Shia, Druze, Maronites, Orthodox, and more . . . I'm sick of living in a country bordering another under Jewish control."

"But will you be able to live abroad," they asked him, "now that you're over fifty and rooted so deeply in Lebanese soil?"

"Yes," he replied. "I could pull up my roots, carry them on my back, and plant them somewhere else—someplace I actually want to live!"

Jawan, in his fifties, emigrated to Brazil—and not because of his financial situation, either.

Flora went back to Lebanon and made her home in Beirut, close to Sawa. Then she got married and, in her fifties, had a son and a daughter. The son went back to Cuba, got married, and had children who are said to have played a part in the Cuban Revolution led by Castro. One of them

1. Djemal Pasha (1872–1922) was an Ottoman military leader and one of the "Three Pashas" who ruled the empire during World War I following a coup in 1913 launched by the Committee for Union and Progress (CUP), the most powerful Young Turks faction.

2. George Hatem (1910–1988) was born in upstate New York to Lebanese Maronite parents. He graduated high school in North Carolina in 1927 and studied medicine at AUB and in Geneva. In the 1930s, Hatem traveled to China and joined the communist movement, later becoming the first foreigner to be granted Chinese citizenship after the CCP victory in 1949.

3. 'Umar bin Abi Rabi'a (644–712) was an Umayyad-era poet, born in Mecca to the Prophet's tribe of Quraysh. He is renowned as a key early figure in the Islamic literary genre of *gházal* (love poetry).

was killed standing his ground against the American landing at the Bay of Pigs in 1961.

Flora always maintained that Sawa's relations with Djemal Pasha the Butcher were no more than a rumor. She said that when Sawa realized how bad things had gotten in the region, she settled her affairs and traveled to China with her son Fares. She invited Flora to join her, but Flora thought it'd be too hard to travel with two children at her age.

Flora also used to say that Sawa did her duty and buried her parent's memento after finding her way to her father's village. She stayed in Beijing until the war ended in the region, then returned to Beirut forever.

Jawan says as much, too.

# Translators' Afterword

In 2011, armed with months of research and dozens of primary and secondary sources in Arabic, French, and English on the nineteenth-century Arab intellectual revival known as the Nahda, Rashid El-Daif penned a remarkable, inventive piece of fiction brimming with historical detail. But he also colored in the contours of the landscape, playfully hyperbolizing with the primary aim of telling a story. In the author's own parlance, the book employs "history in the service of *adab*"—a polyvalent term, whose translations include "literature," "etiquette," and "refinement," that connects over a millennium of Islamic belles lettres and poetry from the age of the caliphs of Damascus, Baghdad, and Cairo, through Ottoman rule, the colonial period, and down to the present day. Unlike Jurji Zaidan before him, El-Daif does not write this historical novel primarily for readers' education, but for their enjoyment as well. Its compelling plot, wit, concision and provocative take on East-West relations are among the many factors that drove us to translate *Paving the Sea*. One way in which we have confronted the novel's cross-fertilization of genres is by including a list of principal characters to guide interested readers between the real-life personalities and their fictitious counterparts (most obviously between the real Jurji Zaidan and the made-up Fares Hashem).

Those who have read *Paving the Sea* in the original Arabic know that El-Daif's narrator often uses first-person pronouns even outside of quoted speech, in such phrases as "our country," "our customs," and "our people." These modifiers are often contextually contingent, reflecting the sensibilities of the characters in the moment as they navigate their turbulent historical circumstances. The cases in which the narrator intends, rather, to direct a comment toward a present-day audience are generally obvious and unproblematic in the Arabic prose. But the act of translation, perforce, complicates matters by unseating the text from its original linguistic environment as well as divesting it of its cultural context. For many who read *Paving the Sea* in English, it may be the case that "our" customs are really *their* customs. The translation strategy of domestication, by which a translator aims to fully adapt the text to the target culture, would consistently privilege "their" over "our"—literally and otherwise—and leave us at best with a loose adaptation of the original material. Such a text would have to compensate for its obfuscation of cultural specificities by inventing new meaning altogether. At worst, the final product would be a confused, almost uncanny distortion of the source culture. It would be a text shorn of almost all practical value. Yet, as readers of literature in translation are well aware, even subconsciously, diving into a novel (let alone a poem) originally written in another language is an experience that is supposed to feel to some extent "exotic" and unfamiliar. Indeed, one of the greatest benefits of reading world literature of any kind is precisely the kind of insight that emerges from gazing through textual windows into other worlds *as well as* from riding out the attendant discomfort and strangeness. To this end, as translators we have made interventions in the text—either by inserting explanatory details and glosses into the prose, or by stepping outside the narrative flow to make sporadic clarifications using footnotes—only in cases where the meaning would be murky or lost altogether on readers unfamiliar with the sociopolitical, religious, and literary particularities of the early modern Arab Levant.

In the case of *Paving the Sea,* Western readers also benefit from the fact that, as the story unfolds, the novel's themes of migration, homesickness, and the perils of assimilation play out against such familiar backdrops as Marseilles and Paris, New York and St. Louis. The novel's spatial progression from the village to Beirut, then on to America by way of Egypt and France, allows us to become acquainted with the characters in their native land before they resolve, amid the watershed transformations of the late nineteenth century, to take to the seas in search of opportunity. This home-abroad boundary is, of course, porous, often in unexpected ways: American missionaries and other Westerners are present in Mount Lebanon from the novel's outset, just as the social networks of Syrian immigrants in the postbellum United States shape the trajectory of the characters' experiences abroad.

We ought to note that, even as the narrator moves deftly across historical periods and between the perspectives of different characters, the novel portrays events from a decidedly male-oriented point of view in a manner some readers might find offensive. This is particularly evident in the realm of sexuality, with which the text frequently engages through the institution of sex work. In our translation, we do not cordon off, whitewash, or draw special attention to the patriarchal (and often hypocritical) attitudes espoused or actions taken by Fares and other characters. This choice is not intended to be a validation of male dominance hierarchies or an exercise in moral relativism, though it cannot be denied that the times were, of course, different: The horizons of possibility available to women in social, political, and vocational life were limited compared to those available to men. We believe that El-Daif's skillful blending of fact and fiction through the substrate of storytelling, and the way his narrator guides us through decades of macro- and micro-level transformation and development, will allow readers to appreciate the nuanced intersections of gender, race, nationality, and class that the characters negotiate as a result of their actions and circumstances, and to form their own opinions without further mediation by the translators.

Translation is always a series of difficult decisions. Yet the task of the translator is complicated further in the case of poetry—for, to quote Paul Valéry, poetry is to prose as dancing is to walking. The prosodic element inherent in verse begs the question of how to translate meaning, form, *and* sound. In a few places throughout the novel where verses of poetry or song lyrics appear, we accompany our translation not with a transliteration of the original sounds but with the Arabic text itself. In these cases we have aimed to render the meaning in clear, natural English, while also allowing readers of all backgrounds to appreciate the aesthetic quality of the words on the page and those who read Arabic to delve deeper, if they wish, into the original sources.

N. R. L. & A. J. N.
Autumn 2025

Satirist, linguist, professor, and novelist, **Rashid El-Daif** is one of the leading voices on the contemporary Arabic literature scene. He has published three collections of poetry and numerous novels that have been translated into more than fourteen languages. Described as the Arab world's answer to Umberto Eco, his works represent a painful break with grand ideologies and grapple with the collapse of the initial project of Arab modernity. El-Daif also teaches creative writing at the American University of Beirut, where he has published four collected volumes of his students' work in addition to supervising five novels.

**Nicholas R. Lobo** is a doctoral student in the Department of Middle Eastern and Islamic Studies at New York University. He earned his master's in Islamic history at the University of Oxford in 2024, and his bachelor's at Davidson College in 2020. He has worked for several years as an Arabic-English translator at the Arab Center in Doha, Qatar.

**Alfred J. Naddaff** is a Knight-Hennessy scholar and PhD candidate in the Comparative Literature Department at Stanford University. He earned his master's in Arabic language and Near Eastern studies at the American University of Beirut in 2022, and his bachelor's at Davidson College in 2019. Now based in Istanbul, he writes for various news publications and researches Ottoman-Arabic cultural entanglements under late modernity.

**Zeina G. Halabi** is a writer, editor, and scholar of modern Arabic literature. Her research explores the contemporary legacy of twentieth-century emancipatory traditions, texts, and figures, with a regional focus on Egypt and the Levant. She is the author of *The Unmaking of the Arab Intellectual: Prophecy, Exile, and the Nation* (2017) and the coeditor of *The Cambridge Companion to Modern Arabic Literature* (2026). She is currently research associate at the Orient Institute in Beirut and the Arabic editor of *Rusted Radishes: Beirut Literary and Art Journal.*

www.ingramcontent.com/pod-product-compliance
Lightning Source LLC
LaVergne TN
LVHW100730260926
848956LV00028B/182